The Diary Of A Seventh Grade Hybrid

I0564751

Lee J. Mavin

The sole responsibility for the content of this publication lies with the author.

Printed in China

Grace Publishing

ISBN:9789881922090

Edited by Sam W Pryor

Cover art and layout by Sam W Pryor

For Charlotte.

I don't remember yesterday.

As much as I strain my mind I can't recall a thing, just emptiness. I opened my eyes this morning and the sun was shining on me. It felt like it had been a long time since I last felt its warmth. I got up, looked around to realize I was in a bedroom. I looked out the window to see a busy street beneath me. Bikes and scooters zoomed beneath trees filled with green and red leaves. Why do I feel so sad when I look at them?

Where am I? I feel so small. I looked in the mirror to see a boy. Was I always this young? I recognized my antennas, two green feathery things sticking out of my head, I've always had those. I paced around the bedroom, finding a photo of my mom. Yes, she's my mom.

I wandered outside and went down some stairs to find my mom in a kitchen. She smiled at me and gave me a glass of orange juice, my favorite.

I told my mom, "I don't remember yesterday."

She gave me a worried look, then guided me into a small living room and sat me down on a sofa. She said, "Ziggy, there is a lot to explain, but it's too early now. Tomorrow, you will start grade seven at Fuqian International High School. I've chosen this school for you for many reasons, which will become clear in the near future."

She handed me a thick notebook and smiled at me. "In order for you to remember, it would be a good idea for you to start a diary. I've been advised to give you this."

So I'm starting this diary at day zero. Zero because I don't know what happened before. I want to remember.

For some strange reason I can write poetry. The words come too easily and I finished one today, thinking of the trees in the streets beneath my room. I wasn't sure if I was asleep or remembering something when I felt the urge to write this:

A Memory or Dream

Where did all the trees go?
Our closest friends have left
Replaced by steel cages
Soil forever wept

Where did all the leaves go?
Burnt in the fire
Their ashes are just memories
Covered with wire

Where did the blue sky go?
Acid storms and flame
Now forever cloudy
Surround us with their games

Where have all the children gone?
Only the elderly linger
On dry lifeless pavements
Death stretches its finger

Monday

Mom told me to write every day, as much as possible so here I go!

It was my first day at Fuqian International High School and I was scared out of my mind. I really didn't want to go and stayed in bed as long as I could. When my mom started banging on my door at 8:06, I knew there was no escaping it.

She yelled, "Now Sigmund, there's nothing to worry about! You know I talked to your principal and teachers. Now hurry up and get ready!"

So I dragged myself out of bed and went to the bathroom. I looked in the mirror to see my antennas stretching. They did this yesterday morning too. They reminded me of sunflowers because they would sag down at night and cover my head, but in the day they would sprout up and tighten which made them harder to hide.

I know I'm different to everyone else. Mom told me to keep my antennas a secret for the meantime and I understand why. If I saw someone like me walking down the street I would probably scream and yell out something like, "Get away from me, Mutant!"

Am I a mutant?

To get back on track, Mom had bought an extra large basketball hat and she squashed my antennas into it. On my way to school I was pretty nervous and I kept thinking my hat would fall off or fly away in the wind, exposing my secret to the world.

I was getting more nervous, when I looked around to see a small boy.

I said to him, "Um, hello, is it your first day too?"

He was actually starting the seventh grade as well, but I thought he looked way too small for high school.

He answered, "Yes, I'm Hiroki. Pleased to meet you," and he bowed.

Straight away I was interested in this small boy named Hiroki.

I said, "I'm Sigmund, you don't have to bow you know."

He smiled to reveal a set of brown braces that covered all of his teeth.

"Oh, I'm sorry, it's a habit I can't get rid of because I'm Japanese."

We walked to school together and straight away I felt less nervous.

Our school was intimidating. Everybody was so tall, and the hallways were filled with busy kids rushing to class.

We had Math first. Our teacher was a fat and boring man named Mr. Brown. After class Hiroki called him *Fatty Brown*.

Next we had Science. It was almost as boring as Math, until the teacher, Mr. Smith, tried to show off and get us all interested in science by turning up the Bunsen burner. He let a huge flame go from a gas tap, but he set his hair on fire! He screamed a little and put it out quickly. Everybody in the class, except Hiroki and I laughed at him. We both thought it was freaky that we were going to use those gas taps in Science every lesson, endangering our hair too!

We then had Gym class, which I actually enjoyed because we played basketball. I wasn't very good at it but I still loved bouncing the ball around and imagining I was a professional player. I noticed a girl watching me when we were playing, I'm sure she smiled at me when I ran past her. She had curly blond hair and looked pretty cute.

Hiroki wasn't bad at basketball, even though he was about the size of a seven year old. He was really fast and could jump surprisingly high. In the end though, our side was defeated easily.

At lunch all the seventh graders kind of stuck together out of fear, and we went to the cafeteria not knowing where to sit.

I heard some big kids say, "Cool! Seventh graders! Look how small they are!"

I heard this other boy, who sounded like a forty-year-old man, say, "I am definitely gonna flush one of them this year!"

I didn't know what 'flush' meant and I did not want to find out.

We huddled like scared mice in the back corner of the cafeteria. We all ate standing up, as quickly as we could, and got out of there.

After lunch we had English, which I loved. Our teacher was young and had curly red hair. Her name was Miss Wood and she loved poetry and creative writing. She wanted us all to write poetry and hand it into her weekly. I'm going to start right away. For some strange reason, I really want to please her.

Finally, the bell rang and we ran home relieved it was all over. I had survived my first day of seventh grade.

Darkness

Before is darkness
Lights ahead
Tunneling outwards
Empty head
Before is nothing
Waste land and sea
Lights ahead
Deaths beneath

Tuesday

I got up early this morning, I wasn't so worried today. Mom made this strange meal, she called it bacon and eggs, but they were burnt, so I couldn't eat it. I drank a glass of orange juice instead, put my hat on tightly and went to school.

On my way to school, I once again found Hiroki following me, and I still couldn't believe he was 12 years old! To me he looked like an infant. He had tiny, skinny little legs that looked like they would break in half if he tripped over. I didn't tell him that though. He was still looking really nervous and I didn't want to be mean.

At school we had Math again with Fatty Brown. It was even more boring than yesterday. Hiroki was caught falling asleep and Fatty Brown yelled at him. He went red and I thought he was going to cry, but he didn't.

Then we had history with Mrs. Wang. She was rather short and had long black hair. She had a funny voice and always said, "Thanking you very much," when someone read something from the textbook. We were studying World War Two which was sort of interesting. I liked reading about war. I especially liked the tactics countries took to take over other countries.

At lunch it was more of the same, 'hiding in the corner like scared mice' again. There were way too many girls in our grade, which only made us look weaker to everybody else.

I hope there's a basketball team at this school! Even though I'm short I still want to play.

I had English after lunch and I couldn't stop staring at Miss Wood. There was something about her that was familiar.

She said to the class, "I hope you've started writing some poetry."

I wanted to show her my first poem, but after reading it, I decided not to. My *Darkness* poem seemed way too depressing for a grade seven class, but I did tell her that I'd written a poem. I thought that maybe I should check with Mom first.

She smiled and I couldn't stop looking at her mouth and lips. Maybe I've met her before ...

That day I walked home with Hiroki. He invited me over to his house, but I said I was busy. I had too much to think about to relax.

Wednesday

A big kid came up to me today and pushed me for no reason. I almost fell over. If it wasn't for Hiroki, who caught me, it would have been really embarrassing. Hiroki was pretty quick, and he could hold me up despite his size.

The big kid just said, "Get out of my way seventh grader!" and kept on walking.

The rest of the day we stuck together feeling scared. Hiroki introduced me to his friend Kane, who was easily the tallest kid in the seventh grade. He was so skinny though, and he had a huge fuzzy ball of hair on his head.

I had been thinking about trees a lot and I found myself calling him *Tree boy,* he didn't seem to mind. When I asked him if he played basketball I was really disappointed when he said he played soccer. He had a really soft voice.

I had to convince him to join the basketball team; he was just too tall not to play!

Kane asked me, "Hey why do you always wear a hat?"

I went red and couldn't answer him. Luckily, after a few minutes of uncomfortable silence, he changed the topic to video games.

After lunch we had boring Math again and I paid no attention.

Thursday

Things got bad! Really bad!

I accidentally bumped into that same boy again today. He said, "Watch where you're going!" and pushed me hard. No one was there to catch me. My hat went flying off my head and out came my secret!

The boy yelled, "Oh my God, what's that on your head?!"

I quickly got up and found my hat. I put it on and ran for the closest bathroom. That's where I stayed the whole day. I kept thinking someone was going to break down the toilet door. I even stayed there an hour after the home time bell went.

I ran home holding my hat down tightly on my head.

I went straight to my room and hid under my covers.

It had only been four days and my secret had been exposed. That big kid was going to tell everyone about my antennas and my life would be destroyed forever.

I hate my antennas! I want to cut them off! Why am I so different to everyone else? Why doesn't anyone else have them? I'm going crazy! I hate my life!

I wrote this poem and read it at loud in my room alone. The words came easily.

Stranger in the mirror

I hide inside
No one is like me
Fire and lies
Shadows behind me
Searching the mirrors
Who am I?
A freak incomplete
On a lonely river

Friday

I faked a cold and refused to get out of bed. I was so red faced that mom believed me. How am I ever going to finish school now? Maybe I could wear a helmet to school. That wouldn't fall off. Maybe I should quit school. I could stay in my room forever and just study. The world doesn't want me anyway! Why should I even bother?

Maybe if I could remember anything that happened last week, I'd find some answers!

Saturday

A strange thing happened to me today. I thought I was asleep, dreaming of Miss Wood's smile.

Suddenly I was standing in a Starbucks coffee shop, waiting in line at the counter. I looked down to find I was wearing a dress. In fact, I felt completely different. I felt like a woman. I ran to the bathroom and was completely shocked when I looked in the mirror … there, staring back at me, was Miss Wood! I touched her long curly hair as if it were my own, and smiled her beautiful smile. I moved around like I was controlling her in a computer game and the control stick was my mind.

I laughed and heard her voice come out of my mouth.

I said, "Hello" and heard her nervous voice echo through the bathroom. "Hello, I'm Miss Wood."

I started laughing more when the bathroom door flew open. A man wearing a suit came in and gave me a strange look.

I realized then I was in the boy's toilets, which would have been fine any other time, but for some reason I had turned into Miss Wood. So I walked back into Starbucks.

I started thinking about being myself again and having those awful antennas and, suddenly, I was in my bedroom again. I was wide awake.

I felt my antennas to make sure I wasn't Miss Wood anymore. Disappointed, I felt them sagging over my forehead.

What had happened? I had no idea. It was crazy!

I decided to see my mom to get my mind off things. She was on the phone with the Principal. She sounded angry.

Finally she hung up the phone and told me, "Now Sigmund, I've spoken with your teachers and the Principal. They assure me that what happened the other day will never happen again."

How were the teachers going to do anything to stop me from being embarrassed every day?

She then said, "That boy Timmy Tang has been suspended for a week, so you don't have to worry about him. If he does anything like that again he will be expelled!"

This wasn't good at all. He got suspended just for pushing me over? That's insane! He's going to want to kill me when he gets back.

Smiling, my mom said, "I chose Fuqian International because I know the staff. It has very high standards for behavior, and the teachers all have connections in high places, if you know what I mean," and she winked at me.

I didn't know what she meant, so I asked, "What do you mean *high places*?"

She nudged me in the shoulder and said, "Oh come on Sigmund don't you remember anything?"

But I didn't remember. I want to remember, but before is still murky. When I try to remember I feel tired, and want to sleep.

Sunday

I'm a kid, but I don't feel like one at all. I don't know why, but I feel different to everyone else. I know the obvious reasons are my antennas, but there is more to it than just that. It must be something to do with not being able to remember. That and the fact that my mom is a little strange too. Hey, come to think of it, what about my Dad? Where is he? I don't even remember what he looks like.

Monday

My mom got me a new (extra large) basketball hat to wear to school, so I had no excuse not to go. But the hat didn't change a thing; I really didn't want to go.

I dawdled around the outside of my house, trying to put it off, but finally I gave up and made my way to school.

Hiroki followed me again, only this time he was tapping on my shoulder *talking to me.*

He said, "I was worried about you."

I asked him, "Aren't you going to ask me about my antennas?"

He replied, "Oh those. We aren't allowed to talk about them. The Principal said if anyone said a word about them they'll be suspended."

That was absolutely crazy! Way too harsh! I thought everyone was going to hate me.

I was wrong. As soon as we got to school kids were saying "Hi" to me. It was weird. In the morning, we walked down the hallway and at least twenty kids I didn't know said, "Hi Ziggy."

Even the older kids were greeting me like they were my friends. I couldn't help but smile when two grade 12 girls said hi to me as we went passed. I felt like a star. Hiroki even gave them a big smile, showing those ugly poo-brown braces to them. I couldn't believe it but they actually smiled back at him. One even said, "Oh, how cute."

In English I felt even weirder. Miss Wood didn't seem her same happy self. Her face was red and she looked as if she'd been crying.

I tried to cheer her up by giving her my poem, *Stranger in the Mirror.*

She gave me a smile and said, "Oh great, thank you Ziggy. I'm very pleased you're putting in a good effort."

For some reason I had wanted a happier response. I don't know why but I had this growing need to please Miss Wood. I wanted to make her happy. I wanted to see her real smile every day.

When I sat back down, I thought about the time in Starbucks. It was so real it couldn't have been a dream. I went on thinking about it in Math and History class. I barely heard anything that Mr. Brown and Mrs. Wang said. I wasn't learning a thing.

Tuesday

More of the same star treatment! Everybody was saying 'Hi' to me again and I was loving it. Tree boy Kane joined in on the fame game and has now become just as popular as Hiroki and I. Other kids were calling him Tree boy too, a nick-name that I made up! We strolled through the hallway as if in slow motion and everyone was looking at us.

I never thought it would be possible. One tiny little kindergarten looking kid, one gigantic boy who looked like a tree and a freak with green things sticking out of his head, becoming the coolest dudes in school. I guess our school was different, maybe we are really cool?

Some of the seventh grade girls were following me around and watching me in class. They'd giggle if I said something and whisper things and giggle more. At first I thought they were making fun of me, but later I realized they weren't.

One of them actually came up to me in the middle of History class and whispered in my ear, "Are you free this weekend?"

I stuttered and said, "Um, yes."

She smiled and replied, "Great, I'm Emily. Here's my cell."

She gave me a little piece of paper with her phone number on it. It had pink love hearts drawn around it. I figured out 'cell', meant 'cell phone' and lots of kids had them.

She stood there waiting for me to say something so I said, "So you want to go to McDonald's or something?" That seemed like a good idea seeing as McDonald's was so popular.

She smiled and looked back at her friends and jumped up and

down as if she had just met someone famous.

She said, "Of course. Call me, OK?" she ran back to her friends who were all exploding with excitement.

Hiroki was sitting next to me completely shocked. I had just agreed to go on my first date ever and it was blowing his mind! He just sat there with the same shocked expression like a robot for the rest of the lesson.

I skipped homework tonight to write another poem for Miss Wood.

Why the café?

Did I dream you?
Or was it real
Spinning mind tricks
Remembering the feel
I was you
And felt at home
I've seen your eyes
From above your nose
I want you to smile
And be pleased with me
Seeking your approval
Secretly

Wednesday

That morning, I went straight to the English department to hand in my poem to Miss Wood. Kids watched me run past and yelled 'Hi' but I ignored them all.

I knocked on the door to find a very sleepy looking teacher holding a mug of coffee.

He said, "Yes Sigmund?" he knew my name but I had no idea what he taught.

I said, "Good morning sir I'm looking for Miss Wood."

He disappeared and then Miss Wood came to the door. She also held a coffee only this one was a Starbucks coffee mug.

I said, "Hey I know you like Starbucks you went there last weekend right?"

She looked worried and moved closer to me, "I was at Starbucks, did you see me there because something weird happened and I can't remember."

I didn't know what to say, "No, I just came to give you this poem for the week."

She smiled but still looked worried, "Thank you for that Ziggy but are you sure you don't know anything about what happened to me at Starbucks? I think I passed out and I can't for the life of me remember what happened. I was waiting in the line and then ... I can't remember a thing."

She smiled and nudged me on the shoulder and for some reason I felt like she had done that before. I said, "It's OK, stuff like that happens all the time."

She then said, "Oh I'm sorry Sigmund; I must sound like a complete nutter right now."

She smiled again and looked into my eyes. She could tell I knew something.

I said, "Sorry I have to go to Math class. It's not as good as your class of course."

I ran off before she could say a thing.

That day I couldn't concentrate. I kept thinking about what had happened in Starbucks. I kept thinking of *being* Miss Wood. I replayed the memory of standing in the Starbucks bathroom, looking into the mirror, in her body.

Hiroki snapped me out of my day dreaming, "Ziggy, you like basketball right?"

I realized we were in the cafeteria and we had somehow managed to get seats.

I looked around to see more grade sevens eating their lunches happily. No one seemed scared anymore. I wondered if it had anything to do with me.

Hiroki clicked his fingers in front of my nose, "Hey, Earth to Sigmund, I said do you like basketball?"

I finally replied, "Yeah of course, you know that."

He said, "Well haven't you noticed the posters all around school for try-outs tomorrow morning?"

"Try-outs!" I knew exactly what that meant.

He took me to one of the posters in the cafeteria.

There it was:

BASKETBALL TRY-OUTS
FRIDAY MORNING
7:30 am SHARP
BRING YOUR OWN SHOES!

I smiled and Hiroki asked Kane, "You going to try out with us Tree boy?"

He waved his head, "No, I told you, I like soccer."

Hiroki seemed frustrated by his answer and told him, "Just come with me and see what you think. You're way too tall to be playing any other sport. Do you know how tall you're going to be?"

He said, "I don't know. My Dad is like 6'5" so I guess I'll be close to that."

"You are underestimating your potential. You are already about 6'1" and you are only 12! You've got a lot more growing to do. Some day you are going to make the NBA you know, and you'll have me to thank when the LA Lakers draft you."

He smiled and I think Hiroki had convinced him. I didn't really need convincing. I was excited to play and test my skills. Though, it feels like a really long time since I've played. I know I love basketball.

Thursday

I spent the whole day just thinking about try-outs. I even took my ball to school to work on my handle. Dribbling was one of my weaknesses.

I was nervous, I could barely remember the last time I had actually played a game of basketball, and starting high school had distracted me completely. I had these fading memories of playing on a team somewhere and wearing a flashy silver uniform, but whenever I tried to remember anymore my mind would go blank until I thought about something else. Somehow I knew that I loved shooting 3 pointers.

Hiroki told me in Math we had a test tomorrow but I was too busy worrying about try-outs to care.

That afternoon we took Tree boy to the basketball court near my place and Hiroki tried to teach him a few things. We quickly found out that he had no idea. He couldn't bounce the ball more than 3 times in a row without it hitting his feet. I was about to tell him to forget about trying out when he jumped up and touched the ring. It was amazing, he could jump!

I tried thousands of times and couldn't even reach the net.

He complained the whole time though saying, "I hate this sport, I want to kick the ball."

But Hiroki kept telling him, "Forget about lame soccer."

I breathed in the fresh air and stared at the trees. It felt good to get outside but I still felt sad staring at the trees. I wonder why?

Friday

Basketball try-outs were crazy. The moment I got there I saw Timmy Tang on the court and I knew I was in for trouble. I played the whole morning with my hat on backwards. My secret was tucked tightly underneath.

Our coach was Mr. Smith. He was also my Science teacher but was a totally different person as a coach. He was yelling at us the whole time so I was freaked out every time I got the ball.

When he yelled, "OK, grade eights play the grade sevens." I was really scared.

Timmy Tang wanted to guard me of course and he pushed me hard so many times. I tried to shoot a few three pointers, but missed them all. No one ever passed it to Hiroki but he tried his best to defend against all of the bigger grade eights. He was actually very quick and one time he almost stole the ball, but he was way too short for any basketball team. Tree boy was disappointing, he played centre and looked like a scared stick-creature that could be blown away in the wind. But I guess the coach would probably pick him anyway just because of his height.

There were a bunch of grade seven kids that were so good I was almost exploding with jealousy. A boy named Wally Foster who was so fast and so good at handling the ball that I thought I was watching a grade 10 play. There were at least 6 other kids who were all taller, faster and better shooters than me. Hiroki was really jealous of them but I liked watching their skills.

Time was running out to impress Mr. Smith so when I got the ball I tried to drive inside. I ran past Timmy and was about to make a cool lay-up when I felt the back of my head fill with a sharp pain. I fell to the ground and looked back to see Timmy Tang laughing.

He said, "Pay back you freak!"

My hat had fallen off and I felt my antennas heating up. Timmy Tang just stood there with the rest of the grade eights and stared at them for a while. I felt the pain in my head go away quickly.

Hiroki lifted me up and said, "Um dude, your things are changing color."

I pulled one of my antennas down to see it had turned purple. I then felt an energy flow through me. But it was too late, try-outs were over and I hadn't made a single shot.

I put my hat back on and we all went and got changed.

That day we had our first Math test and I hadn't studied at all. I didn't have a clue how to answer any of the questions. I ended up guessing them all.

After I was done I looked over at Hiroki and he had answered all the questions. Later he told me the test was easy!

I, however, don't think math is important at all.

Saturday

I went over to Hiroki's place and it was weird. His whole house looked like the inside of a Japanese restaurant. It was all polished wood and paper sliding doors. His mom even wore a Kimono and served me green tea.

Everything was very quiet and we ate lunch in silence. It was yummy though. We ate fish and rice and his parents kept handing us more food and bowing. Hiroki's room was a huge surprise. He had a collection of Samurai swords!

I found out his Dad actually ran a karate school and, unbelievably, Hiroki was a black belt! He said he had been training since he was four years old! I couldn't imagine him kicking anyone's butt though; he was way too small and skinny for that. He did show me some kicks and punches. He could kick above his head which was pretty impressive even though he was only five foot tall.

Hiroki is lucky to have a Dad. Mine doesn't seem to care. I have no idea what he looks like and haven't seen or heard from him at all. I looked around our house, looking for a photo or something, but found nothing.

Sunday

Not much happened. I was dreading going back to school because of Timmy Tang. I knew he wanted to kill me but I couldn't figure out why. The only thing I had done was be myself. Only thing was, being myself made him really angry.

Maybe he's mentally unstable?

Monday

The grade eight kids hated us more than any other grade at school and for no reason. I guess it was because they were older than us and finally they had someone to push around.

I heard from Tree boy, there was this one kid named Jason King who got into a fight with a tenth grader and almost killed him. Apparently he was a part of this gang called *The Meats*. I asked why they were called that and Tree boy said it was because they were all *muscle* and *beef*. He didn't know if Timmy Tang was a member though. I hoped he wasn't. The guy already had enough help to kill me anyway!

I saw Miss Wood that day and she looked like her usual smiling self again. I worked so hard in class to impress her. Hiroki figured out that I liked her and drew a cartoon picture of us kissing. It was pretty well done in the style of Japanese anime but I couldn't let anyone else see it. I quickly tore it out of his notebook and ripped it into tiny little pieces. He just laughed.

Mr. Fatty Brown gave us back our math tests today and he really wasn't happy with my 14% result. I thought it was a pretty good result considering I guessed every answer.

He said, "You're going to have to do much better in the next class Sigmund. You know we set a high standard for every student here. I recommend you study everyday and see me at lunch for some extra tutoring."

This turned out to be a command rather than a recommendation. It was really bad news and I had no excuses not to study more either. I had to agree to the tutoring at lunch, which meant I had to spend double the amount of time with Fatty. As

Tree boy would say, *that totally sucks!*

No free time, Timmy Tang and a bunch of angry eighth graders. I am beginning to hate school altogether.

Tuesday

My first day of double Fatty Math and it was double boring! At lunch he just gave me some extra Math worksheets and sat next to me eating an enormous Subway sandwich. He kept dropping crumbs and bits of meat over my desk. When he talked he spat chunks of his sandwich all over the worksheets. When was I supposed to eat?

I had Math right after lunch so I had to look at or at least smell Fatty Brown for over an hour. All I heard was numbers, numbers, numbers.

That afternoon I tried to teach Tree boy some more moves and Hiroki came along too. Kane was still hopeless but I was surprised at how good Hiroki could play. He was really fast and could handle the ball quite well. He could also jump really high, almost as high as me, and that was pretty amazing considering I was almost twice his size!

Too tired to write anymore …

Wednesday

I sat in the bathroom this morning staring at my antennas. They were green again and were stretching high above my head as if they were trying to reach for something. I noticed the two bald patches on my head where they came out. I frowned at the mirror and put my extra large NBA hat on. Now I looked like a normal kid. But it didn't matter anyway, everybody knew about them.

Then I started thinking, why should I hide them if everybody knew they were there. Everyone was always asking me about them, so maybe if I showed them all they might finally shut up.

I took my hat off and left it in the bathroom. For the first time (at least from what I can remember) I went outside without a hat on. My antennas stretched high up into the sunshine. It felt great!

People looked at me and pointed on the street. Some little kids even got scared and ran away and cried. But I didn't mind that much. I was sick of hiding the real me. *I have two big antennas sticking out of my head! Come have a look!*

When I got to school kids stared at me but not in the same way as on the street. I kind of thought that they were looking at me with respect and when I went to class the respect grew and grew. The teachers didn't seem to even notice, they just went on teaching as if I was a normal kid.

When Hiroki, Tree boy and I walked into the cafeteria together everyone clapped for some reason. I guessed they were clapping for me so I pointed to my antennas and soaked up the attention. Everybody smiled and I was so glad there were some nice kids in this school.

Timmy Tang wasn't one of those nice kids.

He came up to me and said, "You're crazy walking around showing everyone you idiot, sooner or later parents are going to complain and you'll be out of here."

He had three angry looking eighth graders behind him that were nodding their heads, agreeing. We all ignored them and eventually they left.

Nothing much else happened at school.

I wrote this poem thinking about what happened today:

Come and see

Come and see
The weird freak
Yes I feel
And I speak
Come and see
The stranger boy
Can't recall
His first toy
Come and see
The hollow man
Fill him with knowledge
Understand

Thursday

More stares from everybody and more feeling like a star. I was loving it and so was Hiroki. This was probably the first time that he had ever been popular and he had this grin on his face all the time. Even though he had those poo-brown braces girls were giving him nice smiles back all day.

Not wearing my hat to school is turning out great!

I missed out on lunch again because of Math tutoring with Fatty. It was more of the same boring worksheets and watching Fatty eat. This time he finished off two whole cheeseburgers in front of me. When I got home I ate almost half of what was in the fridge.

Friday

I had basketball practice again in the morning and the weirdest thing happened. There was a list up on the wall with everybody's name that had made the team (written in pen). I was so sad because my name wasn't there. Hiroki's and Kane's weren't there either.

I forced myself not to cry and for some weird reason I started to feel sleepy. I closed my eyes.

I opened my eyes to find I was a little taller and a lot fatter. I looked down to see all the seventh grade kids staring back at me. I saw myself sitting down too, only I was asleep.

I had jumped into Mr. Smith's body! I was the coach!

I said, "Excuse me does anyone have a pen?"

Hiroki quickly ran to his bag and came back with a pen. He asked me, "There you are Sir. Are you sure you wrote everyone down for the team?"

I smiled through Mr. Smith's wrinkled mouth and said, "Actually there are some changes I want to make."

I went over to the list and wrote my name, Hiroki's and Kane's. The best thing about it was, it wasn't in my handwriting. It looked exactly like Mr. Smith's writing.

I dropped the pen and woke up in my own body. We watched Mr. Smith stare at the list. He then picked up the pen from the ground and faced us.

He asked, "Hey did I just write these names on the list?"

Most of the kids yelled, "Yes Sir!"

He waved his head looking confused and said, "Well, I must have written them down for a reason. I can't seem to remember… anyway, congratulations to those who made the team, better luck next year for the rest!"

I felt bad for the other kids who didn't make the team. About 10 of them left and there were 13 of us remaining. It was meant to be 10 but I wasn't going to let Mr. Smith make the biggest mistake of his life. All the other kids that had made the team were so tall, but Kane was of course the tallest.

Hiroki was so happy he couldn't stop talking about basketball all day. Kane was also pretty surprised he had made the team too.

I couldn't tell them the truth; they'd never believe it and they were way too happy anyway. Maybe I had set Kane on the path to the NBA!

I went to Math tutoring that day and tried hard to concentrate on the worksheet questions. Fatty was looking upset at me for some reason. He kept frowning at me but didn't say anything the whole time.

I also noticed Mr. Smith in Science class studying my antennas when everyone was filling in a questionnaire. He was also frowning and couldn't keep his eyes off me the whole class. It looked as if he was examining them in some sort of experiment.

He told me, "I see you are growing Sigmund," with this weird smile.

I can't figure out what he meant. I am only 12 and it's still three months until my birthday. My voice hadn't broken yet and I am in no way near growing a moustache. Maybe it is something to do with my antennas?

Note: Be careful around Mr. Smith

Saturday

My date with Emily was scary and weird. I arranged to meet her at McDonald's and she arrived with a ton of make up on. I thought she was trying to be one of the cool girls. She had long straight blond hair and big blue eyes. She was destined to become beautiful, but she was only 12 years old so her pink dress and make-up looked weird. I felt awkward straight away.

I bought her a strawberry milkshake and got myself a large coke. I sat there and listened to her talk about her friends and her teachers. She liked English class and hated Math so I guess we had that in common.

When she started asking me about my antennas, I knew she didn't really like me. She even convinced me to let her feel them under my hat.

She said, "Wow, they are amazing! They feel like flowers!"

I didn't say much after that. We ate some chicken nuggets and I told her about basketball try-outs. She acted really interested and when I told her about Timmy Tang hitting me she seemed really worried.

Then she changed the subject and suddenly and we were talking about my antennas again. I refused to answer her constant questions and things got quiet.

She then said she had dancing class in the afternoon and ran off. I walked back home thinking it was all a waste of time.

I am only 12; I don't really like girls yet. But I guess I do, I like Miss Wood.

My first date was pretty weird and I was disappointed all afternoon. I think Emily only likes me because of my antennas.

Sunday

I spent a lot of time that day in front of the mirror examining my antennas. They didn't look any different and the green feathers seemed the same. They were about the same height but for some reason they felt different.

I asked mom about them but she just ignored me. She always ignored me when I asked her about my antennas. She didn't want to talk much about them at all.

I could move them up and down without touching them and I moved them from left to right in the mirror for ages.

I could even spin them around and twist them up like a tangled skipping rope without using my hands. I think I used to do that when I went swimming. I do remember swimming in some sort of huge swimming pool. The bottom of the pool was see-through and I could see a busy city beneath me, filled with buildings and lights. I think I swam at that pool often. I think I was alone too.

Monday

Our little group of three (Hiroki, Tree boy and I) doubled in size today. Emily brought her friend Janet, and some other really quiet girl with crazy hair who was following them. I asked Emily who she was and she just ignored me. The strange girl was listening to our conversations and sometimes even laughed when Emily tried to be funny. She didn't say a word the whole time.

Her hair was completely insane. It was all curled up in a kind of spiral ice-cream shape on top of her head and was tied up with two red chopsticks.

At lunch I saw the eighth graders giving us evil looks again. I guess more girls in a group would maybe help us not get beaten up. They were our only protection. Surely the grade eight boys wouldn't attack with three girls standing in front of us!

But judging by their angry expressions they looked like they were planning something awful. They are probably going to kill us when we are least expecting it.

We need more protection! We need a miracle!

I forgot all about Math tutoring! I'm going to be in deep trouble!

Tuesday

I dreaded seeing Fatty that morning and I knew he'd be angry. What made things worse was I had Math before lunch! He made me sit at the front and was all red faced as soon as he saw me.

He asked me to answer every question and when I did he yelled, "No! Incorrect again!"

He was right, of course, I was always wrong.

I knew he was trying to make a point, but he didn't have to embarrass me in front of the whole class! Meanwhile, Hiroki was writing down every answer correctly at super speed. It sucks because I never see him studying. I'm so jealous!

At lunch Fatty told me, "I want to see you here, before school, at 7:30am every morning, until your grades start improving."

It's completely unfair! I know for a fact that Kane is doing just as bad as I am, and he isn't doing any extra tutoring! Some other kids are also poor at Math and he doesn't even say a word to them.

If I do this crappy morning Math class, I'll miss out on Friday basketball practice!

I tried to argue with him and said, "Please let me go to basketball on Fridays, I just made the team!"

This only made his face red and he yelled at me, "I think basketball should be the last thing on your mind. You must start concentrating on your studies, it is very important for your future!"

I then said, "But other kids aren't doing well either, and you aren't making them do extra work. Why me?"

His face looked like a red traffic light and it was flashing too! He yelled, "You are not just any child Sigmund! You must learn at a faster rate than any other student as you will soon have bigger responsibilities! You may not realize this now but there are many important individuals tracking your progress and monitoring your growth. In the future you will be required for things that you cannot imagine now! You must not only master Mathematics very soon but you must also master Physics, Chemistry and Economics in the near future!"

I hate all those subjects so I asked, "I'm doing OK in English and History, what about those subjects?"

He yelled, "You needn't worry about those minor subjects, you must focus all your power on Science and Math!"

The dude was a freak. I didn't have a clue what he was on about, but I still worked hard on heaps of his boring Math worksheets.

I walked home that day with Hiroki thinking the school had gone mad. Maybe Fatty had mixed me up with someone else? I can barely pass a grade seven test, mastering the whole subject is way out of my league!

I thought about what Fatty had said. I wondered what 'tracking my progress' meant.

I'm sure Miss Wood isn't crazy though. I trust her.

Wednesday

I didn't sleep well Tuesday night, but I wasn't going to miss my morning Math session again. I was still half asleep when I got there and Fatty had a huge mug of coffee in his hand that I desperately wanted.

I couldn't understand all the things he tried to teach me. All this information was going in one ear and out the other. But apparently I had to concentrate and *progress* so I at least acted like I was interested. It was a very slow morning.

I was so sleepy all day. Hiroki was showing off some of his Karate moves and I barely noticed.

More Math at lunch and I was beginning to see numbers in my head.

122=2131222131513123213412515135 13

I hate numbers! They mean nothing.

Emily hugged me in English in front of everyone. Some kids whistled but I was too tired to even get embarrassed.

That strange girl with the crazy hair was following us around again but I didn't have the energy to ask her the questions I had been dying to ask her.

Thursday

When I awoke this morning I remembered my dream. I was being chased around school by flashing numbers. They were floating in the air behind me and I couldn't get away from them. I tried to stab them with a pencil but that just made them flash more.

I ate breakfast that morning with a pencil in my hand.

That day I heard one of the grade eights say, "We've got to flush Ziggy soon. We are running out of time."

Again with the flush thing, I'm really worried now. I need a plan of defense.

I asked Hiroki about it, he said he didn't know what it means.

My imagination is running wild trying to figure it out. Flush? Why flush me?

Friday

I awoke, realized I couldn't go to basketball training, and was in a bad mood straight away. I dragged myself to Math tutoring annoyed and frustrated. I didn't say a word to Fatty and once again I got most of the answers wrong.

This time Fatty was eating a chocolate bar which annoyed me even more. We call him Fatty for a reason. His gut is ready to explode out of his shirt at any second and his double chin is about the size of the rest of his massive face. It's not a pretty sight at 7:30 in the morning. I'd prefer anyone else, Hiroki, Mom ... even Emily!

I heard from Hiroki and Kane that basketball training was heaps hard and they were tired all day. I'm still jealous though. I was the one that got them on the team and I still can't go to training!

Saturday

Today was terrible! Mom found out about my grades and forced me to study my Math textbook all day. Emily called twice and asked me to go out again but I couldn't go. My life is becoming a constant Math lesson and I hate it. It's killing me!

Sunday

More Math! I hate my life! I'm seeing numbers whenever I close my eyes. I spent the whole day staring at Math worksheets but I hardly learnt a thing. I just daydreamed about playing in the NBA.

Monday

Fatty decided to give us a surprise exam today!

He said, "This is your chance to prove yourself Sigmund."

I hate him.

We started the test and I didn't understand any of the questions. I got frustrated just thinking about all the things I would miss out on if I failed. I thought about missing practice, missing out on dates and missing out on lunch with my friends.

Then I felt dizzy and everything went black...

I woke up and I was in front of the class, sitting at Fatty's desk. In fact, I quickly realized I *was* Fatty, it was happening again! I was fat. I glanced at my arms and legs and touched my double chin. It was totally disgusting.

But, when I saw all the answers to the Math test in front of me, I didn't feel so bad.

I focused all of my energy on the Math answers and something crazy happened. I felt myself jump from Mr. Brown's body to my own body, over, and over again. I wrote down every answer, copying from the answers on the desk. It was like playing leap frog and it was so easy. I felt waves of energy surge through me.

I made sure to answer six questions incorrectly before I was finished. No one would ever believe I would get 100% right.

But that's when I had a funny idea. I jumped back into Fatty's body and stood up in front of everybody.

I yelled, "Class. Please stop what you are doing, I have something to announce!"

49

Everyone looked up except for me; I had my head down on the desk, fast asleep.

I then yelled in Fatty's deep voice, *"I like to party all night long!"*

I tried my best to do a little dance. I even shook my enormous behind in front of everyone. At first they gave me shocked looks, but soon they were laughing, loudly.

I kept dancing and sang, "We don't need no Math. We just like to party. We like to party! We like, we like to PARTY!"

I jumped back into my own body and saw Mr. Brown standing there looking confused.

He said, "Why are you all laughing? Get back to work. This is an exam you know!"

It took a while for everyone to settle down. Heaps of kids couldn't stop cracking up with laughter.

I handed my test into him smiling. Hiroki handed his test in mimicking Fatty's dance. Fatty looked like he had no idea what happened.

Fatty's version of *We like to party* spread throughout the school and everyone was singing it. Thanks to me, Math had become fun for a change.

I realized today that I can control this power. I can use it anytime I want. The possibilities are endless. I can jump into any one's body and no one will ever know!

Tuesday

I slept well.

In the morning Mr. Brown looked impressed and said, "I'm very pleased that all of this extra tutoring and studying has paid off Sigmund. I marked your test this morning and I'm happy to say you got 93%! Great work!"

I reminded him, "So can this be the last morning Math lesson, if I keep getting good marks?"

He nodded and said, "Sure and lunch time is yours again, but, if you fall below 50%, we'll have to have another chat."

Lunch time is mine again! I feel like a weight has been lifted off my shoulders.

I walked into the cafeteria at lunch doing Fatty's party dance and got a little round of applause from my friends.

I'm back!

Emily looked especially pleased.

Wednesday

This morning things were back to normal and I walked to school with Hiroki. My antennas were stretching out in the sun. We walked down Nanjing road and dodged scooters and bikes to get to school quicker. Being free of Math tutoring felt fantastic.

Hiroki filled me in on what I had missed over the week at lunch. Apparently, the grade eights were causing trouble again. They were pulling chairs out from under grade seven kids when they were eating and one kid had a full bottle of coke tipped all over him. One other kid had his cheeks smeared with peanut butter. It was scary stuff. The cafeteria had turned into a war zone.

Luckily our group had remained unharmed in the crossfire. Hiroki told me that Tree boy had ducked a flying apple, and Emily had almost slipped over another kid's lunch that had been thrown on the ground. Apart from that they were surviving.

Today at lunch the grade eights had vanished and there was an uneasy calm in the cafeteria. We ate our lunch with our heads down, fearing the worst.

Thursday

I was happy to go English class today with a clear head. My antennas felt rejuvenated and even seemed a little taller.

I smiled at Miss Wood and she smiled back. Her smile is beautiful and it is enough reason alone to go to school. She's the most beautiful teacher by a mile. I wonder how she became a teacher so quickly; she must have graduated so young!

I can't explain why, but I feel like I know her better than anyone else.

I kept thinking about her all day until finally I couldn't resist ... I jumped into her body again!

I tapped my beautiful fingers on the desk and noticed her handbag sitting under the chair. I reached into it and grabbed her purse. I quickly opened it to find her driver's license which revealed her age, she is 36! She looks way younger than that! Behind her license was a photo of a man wearing a suit and a strange looking hat. I felt really weird looking at his face. I don't know why, but I felt angry.

I jumped back feeling sad. I had always imagined Miss Wood as a single lady, but somehow I knew the guy in the photo was her boyfriend.

That day I also noticed that strange girl following us again. She had been doing this for weeks and I still hadn't heard her speak.

I asked Emily what her name was and she smiled and said, "Oh that's Mary Jiang, she's just really quiet ... but she's really nice. She's a new girl, moved here last month from some other country."

I wasn't convinced she was nice. Whenever I looked over at her she was staring at me. She was always looking at my antennas.

She is short, but her hair is tied up so high that it makes her seem tall. There's something really strange about her, maybe it's just all those curls massed up on her head.

Friday

I went to basketball practice in the morning and I *sucked* badly. I missed every shot and couldn't keep up with all the other, taller, grade seven kids. Tree boy fell over a few times and Hiroki had no idea. I guess we are the three worst players on the team. That makes sense considering we didn't actually make the team anyway.

Mr. Smith was looking worried. He yelled at us, "You're getting it all wrong!"

After practice I wondered if I was ever going to get good. It would take a lot of practice, but I guess I'm only 12 years old. I've still got five years to impress the NBA scouts and five years of growing, at least.

Today in Science Mr. Smith said something strange. He said to me, "We will need to take you in for testing on your upcoming break, I'm afraid it may be uncomfortable at times."

I didn't know what to say. I had no idea what he meant. *More testing*? What a totally random thing to say.

Saturday

I had another date with Emily today, only this time I brought Hiroki, and she brought Janet. I think the double date is way better; I felt more relaxed with Hiroki around and whenever it went silent I just talked to him.

Hiroki was actually really nervous. Before the date he told me he had *a mega crush* on Janet. He didn't say a word to her during the date.

Going to the movies didn't help; Hiroki sat next to me and spent the whole time asking me what Janet was doing.

Emily was whispering in my other ear so I pretty much missed the movie. I even forget what it was called.

It seemed like a very long time since I had been to the movies.

Sunday

I went to the basketball court today with Hiroki and Tree boy. I tried teaching them a few things, but I wasn't that good anyway. We were all still hopeless. Tree boy couldn't even get a shot from under the basket and he was huge!

We played all day and afterwards my feet and knees were aching. I staggered home, ate and went to bed early.

Monday

Emily held my hand in the hallways and everyone looked at us. Some kids even whistled. I felt my face heating up and knew it was red. Still I didn't let go of her hand because it would have embarrassed her completely. She was smiling.

I guess I'm not just a cool kid with two green things sticking out of my head. I'm the cool kid with a girlfriend! I'm only 12 and I already have a girlfriend, it feels bizarre.

Everyone was saying 'Hi' to us so I guess Emily has become popular as well. She looked like she loved it too.

We sat together in Math class which made it harder to concentrate. She kept drawing love hearts all over my book and we didn't get any work done. I guess it doesn't matter because I'm going to pass every test.

I deliberately sat next to Hiroki in English class. I don't know why, but I don't want to be close to Emily in front of Miss Wood. It feels wrong.

Tuesday

I bumped into the grade eight kids again today. Timmy Tang tripped me over too.

He said to me, "Hey freak boy, why are you still here?!"

I told him, "If you do that again, I'm going to tell the Principal and you'll get expelled."

He walked off with his friends trying to act like he didn't care. I knew he did. He wanted to stay at Fuqian High. I'm sure his parents were paying loads of money too.

I'm refusing to be scared of him! The grade eight kids don't know what I can do if they test me. I'll show Timmy Tang who is tough, he'll think twice once I'm done with him.

Wednesday

Our school is a pretty cool place sometimes. Hiroki and I went to the library today and found a huge collection of Japanese comics. I'm talking a whole isle just for Manga! It was great! We sat there reading them the whole lunch time.

Miss Wood gave me my poems back. She put an A+ on the top of each poem and wrote 'Well done!' and 'Excellent Work!' I want to give her more poems, so I'm trying to write some more tonight.

In History today we were given an assignment:

Write about an invention that changed the world: Due Week 10

That means that I have less than three weeks to write it! I thought about some inventions like electricity and the telephone, but decided they were too boring. More things to worry about! In a frenzy of stress I didn't know where to start, so I started writing another poem.

All eyes on me

You look at me
Wondering how
I feel the same
I'm wondering now
Wondering around
Without a shadow
Past is the trash
Future is a sparrow

Thursday

Timmy Tang pushed me over in the middle of the cafeteria today in front of everyone. I spilt rice and veggies all over the floor. I was really angry!

I pulled myself up and looked him straight in the eyes. I told him, "Don't do that again … or else!"

He sniggered and said, "Or else what?" and pushed me again. This time it was really hard. I fell over and hit my head on the floor.

Revenge time! I closed my eyes and opened them in Timmy Tang's body. I bent down and picked up chunks of rice and veggies off the floor and rubbed them in my face.

I yelled, "I'm sorry Ziggy, I'm an idiot'

I pulled his shirt over my head and ran around the cafeteria waving my arms like a bird, chirping "I'm an idiot, I'm an idiot!"

I had everyone laughing so hard they were crying. But I wasn't finished...

I decided to pull his shorts down too and did some dancing, *Fatty* style.

I yelled, "I also like to party like Mr. Brown!" Wearing nothing but an ugly pair of yellow undies.

I finally jumped back to see a red faced Timmy Tang looking completely terrified. He ran out of the cafeteria screaming, trying to pull his clothes back on.

I guess now he'll think twice about pushing me over!

Friday

More basketball training today and more bad shots. Our team isn't very good at all. Mr. Smith told us that we have a game next week and gave us all new uniforms. I chose number five; it was cool to see our new blue and white jerseys. Although the thought of playing a real game freaks me out.

When Hiroki tried his jersey on it was way too big, even though it was the smallest size they had, extra extra small. Tree boy's jersey was too tight and it looked like a tank top with his stomach showing. My jersey fit perfectly!

Even though we were all happy to get our new uniforms, we were still worried about our first game.

That day, school was pretty uneventful.

Saturday

I went over to Hiroki's place again today we ate sushi for lunch and he showed me some more of his Karate moves. He could kick really high too! Way above his head! He even smashed a plank of wood in half with his hand. It was weird, his mom and dad were bowing to me constantly.

After, we went to the courts to practice some more. I know we need it. I showed Hiroki how to do lay-ups and he was slowly getting the hang of it.

That night I talked to Emily on the phone. She said she missed me and I didn't know what to say. There was a huge silence and she sighed. It was heaps embarrassing. But then she convinced me to go on another date without letting me say no.

I can't stop thinking about how nice Hiroki's parents are and how different his family is to mine. I can't remember my father and I'm wondering why he's not around. Could they be divorced? Or maybe even worse, could he be dead? When I get a chance, I want to ask Mom about him.

Sunday

My *real* date

This wasn't just any date, it was dinner. Mom told me that I always had to look my best for dinner dates. She was way more excited than me about the date and she picked out my fanciest shirt for me to wear. I chose to wrap my antennas in a grey bandanna. Mom also told me to buy flowers, so I did.

When I saw Emily I thought she had gone to way too much trouble to look grown up. Her hair was super curly and she wore a red dress that looked expensive. When I gave her the flowers she went crazy!

She jumped up and down in the middle of the restaurant and yelled, "Thank you, thank you, thank you!"

We were at a nice Hong-Kong restaurant in the city and everyone else around us were adults. Men were wearing suits and women were all in dresses and high-heels. I felt weird being the youngest there.

Emily was smiling a lot and wouldn't stop talking. I noticed she had make-up on and it made her look much older.

After we had finished I paid for everything and this made her smile even more. She grabbed my hand on the way home and just blabbed on and on about school. When we got to the front of her apartment she kissed me on the cheek and ran inside before I could say anything.

It was all so embarrassing. Emily definitely likes me, but why? I'm a weirdo. Come to think of it, she didn't say anything about my antennas the whole night.

I'm so glad it's over; I'm not looking forward to another dinner date. For some reason, I'm not interested in her at all. She seems nice enough, but I just think all this is just one big distraction.

Monday

That morning at school everybody already knew about my date! Some girls I didn't even know in grade seven were whispering my name as I passed and gave me strange looks. Yeah, I have a girlfriend! So what?

Actually, I think I'm the only guy in grade seven with a girlfriend.

I got word from Tree boy today that the grade eights were seriously planning to flush me. He said he heard about five of them talking and they were waiting for the right time to launch their attack. What kind of attack?

I had an idea.

Hiroki and I went all the way to the grade 12 area today at lunch to find out more about the whole *flushing* thing. It was scary because they were all so huge. You see, grade 12 kids aren't *kids*, they're fully grown adults. They looked at us like we were babies. I heard a girl say "Oh look, they're so cute."

But we weren't there just to be looked at; we had a mission to complete.

Hiroki took my hand and guided me into a group of long legged girls who were sharing each other's head phones, listening to music.

Hiroki was brave and asked one of them, "Um, hello, we are new and we were wondering what it meant if someone … *flushes* you?"

The girl, actually she was practically a woman, pulled out one of her head phones and said, "Flushing? Wow that's so *old school*.

That's when a kid sticks your head in the toilet and flushes it of course. I haven't heard of that since grade seven."

We were both terrified and got out of there, panicking like two mice running away from a cat.

So now I know what flushing is. It's completely disgusting and insane!

They want to stick my head down the toilet?! Yuck!

Tuesday

I had to take precautions if I was to avoid a *flushing*. That meant not being near a school toilet, ever. The further away from them I am the better! Today I even kept my distance from the outside of the toilets and walked on the other side of the hallway in fear of an attack from behind.

Tree boy warned me, "You know it will probably be a whole group of them, so it will be impossible to stop them all."

But this reminded me of my new found power. I'm working on my own plan, a counter attack! It's purely defensive.

By the way, I'm totally paranoid if you haven't noticed, I can't concentrate on school work at all!

Wednesday

I didn't tell Emily about the whole flushing thing. I didn't want to worry her and I know she'd probably just makes things worse by trying to talk to the grade eights.

If I am ever going to get them off my back I'm going to have to do it myself. It's better to get it over with than to live in fear for the rest of my life.

Emily could tell that something was up though. At lunch she kept asking me if anything was wrong and I just kept lying and telling her I was worried about my history assignment.

Come to think of it, I've completely forgotten about it! It was meant to be about an invention and I haven't planned a thing!

Thursday

I'm really worried. I'll be doomed to fail unless I do something about my history assignment. Hiroki only made it worse today when he showed me what he had done so far. He'd already written about 10 pages of information about the television. He had even drawn illustrations of early TV designs that were amazing, and so detailed.

I couldn't help but be a little jealous. The guy is a total genius. He's going so well in every class and getting high marks in every test.

I'm calling him *The Ninja Assassin* and whenever he gets a question right, (which is always) I'd whisper to him, "Slice that Katana!"

He always smiled when I said it, showing me those huge ugly braces.

Another thing has me worried. Today that strange girl, Mary Jiang, was following me around everywhere. She still hasn't said a word, either. She never smiles or laughs, maybe she doesn't know English well. She is very short, has big brown eyes, really long eye lashes and always has a blank expression on her face. Maybe if she smiled she'd be pretty?

But I don't have the time to go and see what she's up to. I have way too many other things on my mind. And besides, Emily said she is harmless.

I trust Emily ... I think.

Friday

Basketball training again and this time it was really tiring. Mr. Smith was getting angry at me and Hiroki. I can understand why too, we suck! He's not as hard on Tree boy just because he's tall, but he sucks too.

That's the way basketball goes, if you're tall, the coach will always give you more chances to get better, in this case he was giving Tree boy hundreds of chances. I still haven't seen him get one shot in ... and we've had five training sessions!

He is slowly learning to dribble and I guess that's why Mr. Smith is more lenient on him, he sees potential just like Hiroki and I do.

Today I got through another day without even seeing Timmy Tang, or any other eighth grader. I haven't used the school toilets all week and I'm taking all the precautions I can to avoid being attacked. I don't drink much during the day, for obvious reasons, and I'm paranoid out of my mind.

Once again I didn't learn or remember a thing.

Saturday

I felt a little sick today, also my muscles were aching from training yesterday. I didn't have the energy to leave home. I just stayed in my bedroom all day and read a bunch of Manga comics. I tried to do some research on the internet for my history assignment, but fell asleep at my desk. I had this weird dream. It was like I was watching a News program on TV, or something, about a crazy invention. It was a cool looking car that ran on garbage and could transform into an airplane. The reporter called it, "The greatest invention of the decade' and when I woke up I couldn't get the image of the car out of my head.

I started drawing it and for some strange reason I could draw it really well. I could even draw the motor pieces in detail. I drew all the individual parts for hours, and then I fell asleep again.

Sunday

I felt worse today. I had gone to sleep without dinner and mom was really worried. We couldn't go to the doctors because of my antennas; well that's what mom has been telling me. I guess I believe her. Mom has all the medicine I need at home and this is the first time I can remember ever getting sick. In fact I can't even remember ever having the flu!

Mom always calls me the *Super Kid*, but I can't do anything super, well actually now I can. I wonder if anyone else can.

I drew more and more today, I filled my whole room with sketches of the flying car.

I'm sitting back staring at them now and it's really weird. Maybe I'm going crazy?

Monday

Tree boy told me today that we have our first game this Saturday.

He looked freaked out when he said, "I don't want to play, I need way more practice, I'm just gonna sit on the bench."

I don't want to sit on the bench! I want to start and score every point! Somehow I think that's not going to happen. There are at least seven guys on our team that are taller, faster and more skilled than me … I hate them all.

In Math today I was getting weird looks from Fatty Brown. He wasn't looking at my antennas; he was kind of looking into my eyes. He nodded a few times and for a moment I thought he was looking into my mind! I felt his sweaty stench and heaviness in my head for a few seconds and then it was gone and he went on teaching the class.

It creped me out all day. Maybe I imagined it? I don't know, maybe I need more sleep.

Tuesday

Takeshi Shibuya invented the first garbage powered, flying automobile in the year 2028. He was one of Toyota's top robotic designers for over two decades and worked on several robot prototypes that were eventually used in hospitals and nursing homes all over Japan from the year 2019. He was awarded the Nobel Prize for Science and Technology in the year 2030.

I don't know why but I can't stop writing about this Takeshi Shibuya guy. I have this voice in my head telling me all this information like a news report. I wrote pages and pages of information about his flying car and robots.

I'm going mad!

This is scary stuff! Today on the internet I looked up Takeshi Shibuya and the Toyota Company, and he actually exists!!! He is 30 years old and was born in 1979. I read that his job is the Assistant Director of robotics!

Is the voice in my head from the future?

Wednesday

Back at school I saw Timmy Tang again. He didn't say anything, just smiled and raised his eyebrows as if to say, 'We are gonna get you!'

Why is grade seven so hard!? I'm never going to live to see grade eight, I'm way too weird to be left alone. I'm a big target for every bully in the school and nothing is going to change that.

I know an attack is going to come soon.

I told Hiroki about it and he just shrugged his shoulders. Hey, the Ninja Assassin could kill them all! No wait that's impossible, he's way too small.

I sat between Hiroki and Emily at lunch with my hat on, eating in fear. I was sweating all day.

But I'm here again, I survived. Untouched and unflushed for another day!

Thursday

I took my basketball to school today and we practiced. Hiroki, Tree boy and I were all way too excited about the game. I even managed to teach Tree boy how to do a reverse lay-up. It wasn't too hard for him, because he was a giant. His style was still ugly though.

In History class we worked on our assignments. As soon as Mrs. Wang told us to get to work, I started hearing that News reporter voice again. He was going on and on about Takeshi Shibuya, so all I could do was write it all down.

The NurseMate 100 was the innovation that the world's ever-growing population desperately needed. It was ready for production in the year 2019 and was available for use in most hospitals from 2020. The NurseMate 100 had the ability to carry, feed and help patients use the toilet. It also had the ability to check their heart rate and even record and measure their brain activity. This model alone propelled the Toyota company into the highest earning enterprise from 2020. They remained the top profit earners for the next 10 years.

I couldn't stop writing and the voice didn't stop until school was over. I drew some designs of the NurseMate 100 and when Hiroki saw them he fell out of his chair because they were so good.

I don't know why, but I can suddenly draw really, really well.

Friday

At basketball training we got the bad news. The starting five was announced and the three of us were of course, not in it.

Starting Centre: Sam Zhang
Starting Power Forward: Jacky Kibata
Starting Small Forward: Jimmy Brus
Starting Shooting Guard: David Myers
Starting Point Guard: Wally Foster

I'm especially jealous of Wally Foster. He is so fast no one can catch him. They are all great players and they're all way taller than me. Tree boy is the only one taller than Sam Zhang, but unlike Tree boy, Sam Zhang can actually catch the ball and bounce it.

But I still believe in Kane. He'll improve slowly. I, on the other hand, am doomed to be short forever!

We watched the starting five do drills and I thought I'd never be better than them. They were like mini NBA players! It totally sucks!

Our first game is tomorrow and I know I'm not going to get any court time because I'm too crappy for Mr. Smith to give me a chance.

That day Emily told me she will come to our game. She said she'll cheer us on. This annoyed me. It will only make things worse. I begged her not to but she seems determined to embarrass me to death.

In Science another weird thing happened. Mr. Smith gave me a huge thick textbook titled, *The Universe*.

He whispered to me, "It's time you started studying your extra subjects. Astronomy is the most important of these ... for obvious reasons. I need you to memorize the Milky Way by the end of this week."

Memorize the Milky Way! How is that even possible! Why do I have to do all this extra work? Mr. Smith is starting to sound more and more like Fatty Brown, which can't be good for my chances on the team. Everyone is turning against me.

Thank God for Miss Wood!

Saturday

"*Bench Boys* in the house!" That's what Tree boy kept saying.

Our first game was a complete disaster! Let me start with the first quarter. We didn't score until there was only three minutes left. By the end of the quarter, the score was 24-4. Hiroki, Kane and I were watching in embarrassment from the bench. We were playing Fudan International School, so their players were from all over the world. They were great shooters and were even too fast for Wally Foster. But Wally was the only guy scoring for us, which made it even more impossible for me to get any court time.

The second quarter was more of the same. They defended us well, we'd turn the ball over and they'd score again. By half time the score was 52-12 and Mr. Smith still hadn't even looked at us.

In the half time break, Mr. Smith just talked to the starters and wrote up some plays on a clipboard, like the NBA has. I didn't have a clue what he was on about anyway.

The third quarter was a complete blow out. We only scored four points! They just kept running past us. Lay-up after lay-up.

I heard Emily yell out, "Put Ziggy on!"

But Mr. Smith wasn't listening to the crowd, which consisted of three girls and my mom.

At the start of the fourth quarter, I was shocked when Mr. Smith turned around to us and subbed in Kane for Sam Zhou. He was easily the tallest guy on the court but the other team started laughing and saying stuff about his fuzzy hair.

Wally passed him the ball and straight away he took the worst shot I've ever seen. He threw the ball way over the backboard and it hit the wall behind the court, hard. I couldn't sit there and watch anymore. I focused all my energy on Kane and suddenly found myself on-court, in his huge body. Wally passed me the ball and I ran past two defenders and scored an easy lay-up. I got the ball again and shot an outside jump shot, and it went in! They kept passing me the ball and I kept scoring. I think I scored at least 10 points. Finally the buzzer went and the final score was 60-24, still a horrible result.

I looked over to the bench to see myself asleep. I quickly jumped back into my own body.

Kane looked at me, confused.

He said, "Did I just fall asleep? Did we win?"

I told him, "No, but you scored 10 points! See, I told you you could play!"

He smiled, still looking confused.

Sunday

I felt really tired and stayed home. I read some comics and I also started reading that Astronomy book. I read a couple of pages and, thinking I had read it all before, I fell asleep.

Not much else happened. Emily called and that's about it. She sighed a lot on the phone and there were a lot of silences. I didn't know what to say to her.

Monday

Things got a little crazy today … I was saved by a friend in the last minute though.

The grade eights had planned an attack for me and Timmy Tang was obviously the one behind it all. Three really strong kids grabbed me by the arms and legs and carried me towards the toilets. I tried to break free, but they were way too strong for me.

I heard Timmy Tang behind them saying, "Quick! Before anyone else sees!"

But someone did see, and totally stopped them.

Hiroki, the smallest kid in the school, came to my rescue. He knocked down three of the grade eight kids holding me with some kind of super karate round-house kick. Then, he swoop kicked Timmy Tang, and tripped him over. It was like a scene out of a kung fu movie!

But that's where the action ended because we made a run for the cafeteria. Thankfully the Principal was lining up to get food! So the grade eights stopped at the door and tried to act like nothing happened. We both lined up in the lunch line, puffing and red faced. The grade eights disappeared.

I can't believe how brave Hiroki was. I owe him now. I owe him big time!

Tuesday

Today Miss Wood showed up to class with a new hair style. She had straightened her hair and it made her look even more beautiful. For some reason, her new hairstyle looked familiar, maybe I've seen it before. I spent the whole time just staring at her. Luckily Emily didn't notice, she appeared to be busy working ... for a change.

I'm thinking about Miss Wood all the time now. She's in my dreams too. I feel like I know her so well even though she's just my English teacher and we've only known each other for less than nine weeks! It's crazy, but I can't help it. She makes me smile.

I even told her today, "Miss, I like your new hairstyle."

And she smiled and replied, "Oh thanks Ziggy, I knew you would. You know, you're the only one who noticed."

And then, she gave me that smile I loved.

I realize now that this is a big problem. Having a crush on your English teacher is one thing, being in love with her is another, especially when I already have a girlfriend!

This must remain a secret.

Wednesday

Takeshi Shibuya robotics and the Toyota Company bought-out the World Military Organization in 2031. He designed eight new Robot Soldier prototypes that would soon defend the earth from its inevitable invasion. Billions of dollars were spent to perfect the prototypes. They were equipped with energy cells that ran on water and had the ability to fire projectiles that were intended to trap their enemies. At the time little was known of the enemy, so these robots were invented to capture the enemy alive. They proved ineffective after the second and third attacks.

The voice in my head was non-stop today. Takeshi Shibuya was turning out to be a very important person ... but what does it have to do with me?

Thursday

Hiroki is now at risk from an attack from the grade eights. We only have one more week until our two week holiday, and we must be cautious in order to survive.

Today I told Hiroki to stay away from all of the toilets, and he did, just like me. He is scared and I feel like it's all my fault.

Also, I have been lying to Tree boy all week about the game. He didn't have a clue what happened when I jumped into his body.

I just said, "You played like Shaq" over and over again. I could tell he didn't believe me, even though he nodded his head.

Some friend I am. I lie and put them in danger.

Friday

I still felt guilty this morning so I kept passing the ball to Hiroki and Tree boy in training. One time I was totally open, under the basket, and even then I passed it way out to Hiroki. He shot for a three, but totally air-balled it.

Mr. Smith looked really stressed out when training was over. He said we had another game on Saturday, versus Livingston International School. He also told us they won the whole competition last year, and were much better than Fudan International. This basically means we are going to be smashed.

Mr. Fatty Brown also told us that we have an end-of-term exam on Monday, and it is on all we had learnt the whole term. Only thing is, I haven't learnt anything.

I hate Math.

Saturday

I looked around my room today and, I now realize, I am going insane. I had drawn designs of cars and robots all over my room like a mad man. I had also written over 50 pages of information on Takeshi Shibuya's inventions. I don't know why I keep doing it, but I feel I need to listen to the voice in my head.

Whenever I hear it I go into a trance and write faster than I can normally write. I'm sure if someone saw me they'd freak out.

Today's game:

We got our butts kicked again. But a crazy thing happened; Mr. Smith actually gave me some court time! It was only three minutes, but I still managed to shoot two shots in that time ... both missed.

Sunday

I had another date with Emily today, even though I should have been studying. It was really weird because all she did was ask questions about my antennas. She seemed a little different today, too.

I was starting to get upset about all the questions, when her voice went all croaky and she got angry. She reminded me of a frog, if they could talk.

She yelled, "You must give me more information. More information is required!"

I didn't know what to say, so I just made an excuse and ran home. Like some scared little kid.

Maybe Emily isn't what she makes out to be. I think she wants to act innocent but I don't know what she's really thinking. It could be anything! I don't know what's behind those big brown eyes.

Monday

My last week of term one started out horribly. I had my end of term Math test and I didn't have a clue AGAIN! I completely forgot about jumping and just tried to do the test like a regular kid. Turns out I'm a regular stupid kid. I'm doomed to fail Math forever.

Hiroki was looking like a Whiz-Kid as usual. This time I'm super jealous. I respect him now too because I know him better, and I'm just amazed at how good he is at every subject. The only thing he sucks at is basketball, but I suck too.

But the dude saved my life!

I spent half the exam just thinking about how amazing Hiroki is.

The rest of the day I kept noticing strange Mary following me. Today was different though because I turned around and finally confronted her.

I looked her straight in the eyes and asked her, "Why do you keep following me?"

She said, "Why is irrelevant. What is important is your safety, Sigmund Zhou. You need to be more careful."

I asked her what she meant and she just frowned and said, "The enemy is closer than you think. I'm here to make sure you stay safe."

So, turns out, I might have some weirdo following me around. I have no idea what she meant. I wonder why she would say such a ridiculous thing.

Tuesday

Today I got the worst news ever. I failed the Math test and Fatty wants me to do extra morning tutoring again! It totally sucks. He kept going on about the importance of studying so I just kept nodding away. I guess next term is going to be just as crappy as this one. More math!

I also forgot entirely about the History presentation. Hiroki's presentation was, of course, brilliant. I thought he was going to do something about the Television but he had changed his mind at the last minute. He brought a katana to school and talked about the invention of the sword. He spoke so confidently. Everyone enjoyed it.

There were lots of other interesting presentations and I was getting really nervous when my turn was coming up.

When Mrs. Wang called my name I froze. I didn't know what to do. I reached into my bag, grabbed a bunch of papers, and walked up to the front of the class with them. I realized, when I looked at the papers, I had taken the pictures of Takeshi's flying car with me. I started talking about it and couldn't stop.

I said, "Takeshi Shibuya's water powered car completely changed how the world used energy. Soon after, petrol powered cars were completely phased out and the effects of global warming were immediately reduced."

I went on and on, listening to the voice in my head. Everyone probably thought I was crazy. Hiroki looked confused when I sat back down next to him.

After class I was shocked when he said, "I have an uncle named Takeshi Shibuya, in Japan, and he also works for Toyota!"

This blew my mind. Could Hiroki really be the nephew of the same Takeshi Shibuya I had been hearing so much about?

After school I got some more answers. Hiroki didn't know much about Takeshi's job, but he did work for Toyota Robotics, and he was 30 years old, which meant he was born in 1979!

Crazy, crazy, crazy stuff!

Wednesday

I had way too much to think about to hear even a single word from my teachers today. Except, of course, Miss Wood. I handed a new poem into her, and she smiled that beautiful smile.

I realize I need to figure out what the hell is going on. I kept asking Hiroki questions about Takeshi Shibuya but he didn't know much more.

He was as freaked out as I was when I showed him some of the pictures that I had been drawing.

Maybe I met Hiroki for a reason?

Maybe I'm meant to meet his uncle for some reason too?

I didn't tell Hiroki about the voice in my head. I'm still not ready to tell anyone that.

Thursday

I'm starting to think showing my antennas was a mistake. Ever since I did it, I've had nothing but trouble. It's too late now anyway, even if I wear a hat to school now everyone will know there are two massive green things hiding underneath.

Over the holidays I'm going to find out everything I can about the school too. Fatty Brown acts like he's known me since I was born, and all the other teachers (apart from Miss Wood) are acting way too weird for my liking.

Friday

The last basketball training of the term was today, and I was finally getting some shots in. It didn't matter anyway because Wally was playing way too well for anyone to notice my improvement.

I suggested to Tree boy and Hiroki that we should practice every day of the holidays and they both agreed.

Mr. Smith was giving me weird looks after training too. He didn't say anything to me, but he kept staring at me for ages. He was thinking something about me, I could tell.

Emily was nagging me again about my antennas. After I ignored every question she finally changed the subject to dates on the holidays.

She said something like, "Oh we should go to the Museum, they have some interesting artifacts there," but I wasn't focused on where our next date would be. I have way too many other things to worry about. The grade eights are planning another attack and I can't rely on tiny Hiroki to protect me all the time.

I guess I had survived the whole term, which is something.

Maybe I was just lucky?

The Abduction

I haven't written in this diary for at least two weeks. Don't assume I'm lazy; I have a very good reason for missing all those days. I was kidnapped!

I've just been returned home after, what felt like forever, being held against my will.

(Before I tell you about my abduction, which was completely crazy, I'll tell you another weird thing. When I got back, Mom didn't seem worried at all! It was almost as if she knew it was going to happen. I kept yelling at her and she just kept acting like everything was fine. She wouldn't call the police or anything! So here I am, in my room, with a few hours to write about the scariest time of my life!)

I think it was the Saturday after the last day of term when they took me away. I was standing outside in the morning, bouncing my ball, when someone hit me from behind. I woke up in what I thought was a hospital bed. My antennas were tied up in these red and blue wires, and tubes were sticking into them, sucking blood out!

I didn't have any energy to move at all, so all I could do was sit there and scream.

Soon, two men in white coats came into the room and told me to calm down.

One said, "You have nothing to fear Sigmund Zhou, we are just monitoring your progress."

The other pressed some buttons on a machine next to me and straight away I felt sleepy.

When I woke up they were injecting needles into my arms. There was nothing I could do but watch. I saw them writing something on a clipboard, but then I fell asleep again.

This went on forever. Needle, after needle, after needle, after needle.

I was being monitored. They were looking into my brain, trying to figure me out. They were constantly taking samples of my blood, and were keeping me drowsy with drugs.

I thought I was going to be there for the rest of my life. It was like a horror movie.

A long time after, I recognized some one's voice when I was half asleep. I forced my eyes open and saw Mr. Fatty Brown in a white coat.

He said to me, "It's OK Sigmund, this will be all over soon."

He injected me with more drugs so I couldn't ask him what in the world was happening to me.

Soon after, I was blindfolded and driven back home.

So much for a holiday! I'm still drowsy from all the drugs.

Wednesday

I found out from my mom today that I had slept two days straight after writing my last entry. I still don't have the strength to get up out of bed so, of course, I can't go to school.

Today I slept more and ate a lot. Mom sat by my bed and fed me whenever I woke up. I feel like an injured cat.

I miss Hiroki and Tree boy. I wonder what they are doing at school.

I'm sure Emily is worried sick about me too.

I want to see Miss Wood; she'll make me feel better. She'll understand.

Thursday

I can move around a little now. I'm still not ready to go back to school but I'm getting better. I had a look in the mirror and my face looked like a ghost, I'm so white.

My antennas were saggy and brushing against my head whenever I stood up.

My legs feel like jelly, it's like I need to learn to walk all over again.

I tried to open my Math book to do some studying, but fell asleep after reading a few numbers.

Friday

There was no way I could go to basketball training today. I can't even stand up for more than five minutes at a time.

At least today I could read a bit more. I didn't study though, I just read Japanese comics.

I slept more too.

Saturday

More of the same; eating, sleeping and reading. Emily called me and I said I was fine, apart from that, the day was totally boring.

I can walk a little more and stand up for a bit longer.

I did have enough energy to write a poem, this is for Miss Wood:

Away from you

For far too long
Away from you
Feels so wrong
A stranger without you
On the road alone
Can I message you the truth
Through the interphone

Sunday

I finally felt a bit better and didn't sleep the whole day. I walked around the apartment, stretched and studied as much as I could. I'm so relieved the drugs are finally wearing off. My antennas are looking healthier too and my face is regaining some color.

Monday

I wanted to go to school so badly today but mom didn't let me. She said I needed just one more day rest.

She knows something about my abduction. I can tell when she is lying.

I'm going crazy staying inside but I guess one more day can't hurt. I never thought I'd write this, but I really want to go to school. It's way better than staying home all day.

Tuesday

I finally went to school today. Mom drove me because she was still, supposedly, worried.

Everyone was staring at me again, probably wondering where I had gone. I wore my hat because I didn't feel like having people stare at my antennas.

It was great to see everyone at lunch, in our normal cafeteria spot. Emily wouldn't let go of me.

I told everyone I had been really sick. Everyone except Hiroki, I told him the truth. Not just about the abduction, about everything.

At first I thought he didn't believe me, but then the look on his face became deadly serious.

He's a real friend, I could tell because he really looked worried.

He told me, "I'll do my best to figure out what's going on with the teachers. I know something weird is happening. I'll keep my eye on Fatty for you."

It feels good to have some help.

Wednesday

We were concentrating too much on the teachers today and we totally forgot about the grade eights.

The attack came at lunch time and even Hiroki's black belt in karate couldn't save us.

At least ten kids carried me and Hiroki towards the toilets; I was still too weak to handle even one of them.

Timmy Tang was their leader; he was shouting orders like a drill sergeant.

They took us both to the girl's toilets, next to the cafeteria and forced us into two cubicles.

I had to do something to turn the situation around. I quickly jumped into Timmy Tang's body and yelled, "Wait, stop!"

I pushed two kids away and took my own body in my arms.

I said, "Sigmund is really a cool guy, we should be flushing me instead, I'm the real idiot!"

I then pushed everyone else aside and dumped my head into the toilet. It was worth the embarrassment.

I wasn't finished there. I jumped into another grade eight's body and ran to the next cubicle where they were holding Hiroki.

I yelled, "Hey everyone, let's flush ourselves! It's cool!"

Hiroki stepped out of the cubicle looking shocked. I heard Timmy Tang moaning in the nearby bowl.

Two other really stupid grade eight kids actually flushed their own heads in other cubicles. The rest of them ran off in horror, squealing like piglets.

I jumped back into my own body and flushed the toilet on Timmy Tang's head! I heard him cough, hopefully swallowing some water. It was great.

We ran to the cafeteria, hearing girls scream behind us.

Thursday

I told Hiroki about my extra Math classes and he thought it would be a good idea if he spied on us, just to see if Mr. Brown was up to anything.

It turned out to be a good idea. Hiroki saw something really weird that morning. He said that Fatty was holding this little computer thingy behind his back. At first Hiroki thought it was a calculator, but when I was reading he held it over my head and it flashed a red light. He could see my antennas through my hat for a second, and then Mr. Brown was typing something on it.

We decided we needed to get our hands on that little computer thingy and that it would possibly expose the truth.

I completely ignored Emily today and made more plans with Hiroki. She didn't look happy about it, I don't know why but I feel like I shouldn't be spending too much time with Emily. It makes me feel uneasy. I kind of shake when I'm around her for too long.

Friday

No basketball training for me and Hiroki today, we were busy trying to uncover the truth. Hiroki said he saw Fatty Brown do the same thing with the computer thingy, only this time he was spending more time typing on it. Hiroki managed to get a little closer and he says he saw strange symbols on the computer, definitely not English. He said that the keys glowed green, and the screen was as thin as paper. The weirdest thing was, he said, it disappeared when I looked up at Mr. Brown.

These were Hiroki's words, "It just vanished!" and I believe him.

It sounded way too expensive and advanced for a Math teacher, that's for sure.

Tree boy Kane was actually starting to like basketball. He said he had fun today. I'm so jealous because I know he's going to pick it up so quickly and it's all because of me and Hiroki that he's playing the best sport in the world and not lame soccer. Kane is also a giant, so it won't be long until he'll be dunking the ball with ease. I'm expecting at least 4 million in cash when he signs with an NBA team in seven years.

Saturday

I went into another weird trance today and heard the voice again. This is what it said:

After the Toyota Company became the world's leader in Military production it soon gained political strength. With its worldwide strength spreading to all corners of the globe Takeshi Shibuya was elected President of Earth's Defense Force: an organization created to stop the further invasion and destruction of Governments and people.

I wonder why the voice isn't talking about flying cars anymore.

I still haven't got any replies from Hiroki about his uncle.

Sunday

I finally went out with Emily today. She was being a chatterbox again. She went on and on about school and how *peculiar* it was. She even said, 'I'm so fascinated with the Science taught here. It's seems technology has a long way to go.'

She held my hand as we walked through Xuijia Hui shopping mall.

We looked at dresses in stores that were way too mature for Emily, but she seemed to think she was all grown up. In one (expensive) store she tried on the smallest size of almost every dress. I was bored out of my mind.

I guess I have to do boring things to keep a girlfriend. Do I really want her as a girlfriend? I don't know. It feels wrong going on dates with her.

Actually, I'm thinking about breaking up with her. I just need to wait until the right time to do it.

Monday

I had my hat on tight today in my Math lesson with Fatty Brown. I kept my head down the whole time in the hope of getting some answers from Hiroki, who was spying on us again.

Hiroki told me afterwards that Fatty had put that computer thingy up to my head and it lit up my head like an x-ray! He could see my skull and antennas and he said it looked like there were bones inside too.

We decided we needed to do some more spying to try and get our hands on that computer thing. At lunch, we went to the Math staff room. There were way too many teachers in there to just go in and steal it, but I had a plan.

I jumped into Fatty's body and looked around for the computer. I opened up his suitcase and found it there. I took it to the door where Hiroki and I were standing and handed it to him. Then I walked back to Fatty's desk.

I jumped back into my own body and we ran to the cafeteria.

So now I've got the Doughnut Scanner, well that's what Hiroki called it, I guess because it's round and he's always hungry. It's in my hands now and I'm trying to figure it out. Pressing the buttons isn't working. It's just flashing red.

Tuesday

This morning I woke up early to the door bell ringing. My mom came into my room and told me to get dressed quickly.

I found Fatty Brown standing in my living room. He said, "I believe you have something of mine Sigmund, I ask that you return it to me immediately."

I was too scared to refuse and ran straight to my room and got it. I ran back and handed it to him.

Now I know something weird is going on. How could he know that I took it? Does he know about my jumping?

When I told Hiroki about it he was freaked out too. We both agreed that we need more help so we told Tree boy everything. He said he'd do anything to find out what was going on, and seeing as he hates Math just as much as I do, and thinks Fatty Brown is an idiot, I'm sure he'll be a good help.

Surely the three of us can get some truth out of these freaky teachers. Tree boy also said he'd keep an eye on Mr. Smith at training. I'm sure he's up to something too.

Wednesday

It was a good idea to tell Tree boy. He's already found some crazy stuff out. Mr. Smith isn't what he seems.

Even though Tree boy is huge, he still managed to sneak into the P.E. staff rooms and saw Mr. Smith using a device which sounds exactly like Fatty Brown's computer. He was only there for a few seconds and then he had to make a run for it before being seen.

So it's obvious that Mr. Smith and Mr. Brown are connected in some way. It has to have something to do with my antennas.

We went through all the teachers we knew, trying to figure out which ones could be a part of the *Freak Squad*. All the Math teachers could be in on it, as well as the Science teachers.

I ruled Miss Wood out, for obvious reasons, but there were some other English teachers I know who could have been behind my abduction.

Thursday

Mary Jiang and her mass of curls had been watching the three of us all week.

When I was buying a can of coke she tapped me on the shoulder and said, "You are playing a dangerous game involving Hiroki and Kane. It would be wise to concentrate on your studies. There is little time left."

I just pushed her away and went to English. She followed me into class and sat behind me.

Miss Wood came to my desk half way through class and asked me, "Are you OK Ziggy? You still look a little sick."

I told her I'd had the flu over the holidays, but I wasn't sure if she believed it.

After everyone had left the class, I stayed back and asked Miss Wood if anything weird was going on with the teachers.

She frowned and looked really worried. She asked, "What do you mean?"

I told her that Fatty Brown was asking me to study more and that he was acting strange.

She just smiled and said, "I can keep an eye out for you Ziggy, if that's what you want me to do. Don't worry; I'm making sure nothing will happen to you. You're way too special for that!"

She hugged me and I felt myself go all red. I wanted to hug her back but I was too nervous. It was the best hug ever! For some strange reason I thought she had hugged me before.

I went home telling Hiroki and Tree boy about what happened with Mary Jiang and Miss Wood. They couldn't figure any of it out.

Friday

I really like Miss Wood. I mean really, really, really, like! I know it's impossible, but I don't care, I can't help the way I feel. I know it's not fair to Emily but I'm never going to tell her, and sooner or later we are going to break up so it won't matter anyway. I just need something to happen so I can have a good excuse to end it.

This all sounds cruel but I really don't want a girlfriend, especially Emily. I feel like we are way too different, and she's really just a wannabe 16 year old. I don't always find her annoying, but I can't say I actually enjoy our dates.

But I still don't have the guts to tell her the truth. I held her hand today and didn't say a word to her.

Hiroki knows all about this and kept waving his head. Thankfully he hasn't said anything to her. He knows I'd kill him if he did.

Tree boy said he saw Mr. Brown and Mr. Smith talking today. He said he heard my name being mentioned a few times, but he was too far away to hear anything else.

So this basically confirms that they are working together, and were probably behind my abduction.

I'm glad I've got Tree boy on my side.

Saturday

We had another game today and even though Mr. Smith said I couldn't play, I went anyway and forced myself onto the bench. Didn't matter though, we still lost.

I hardly even saw the game; I was busy concentrating on Mr. Smith to see if he did anything weird.

After the game, Hiroki said he saw Fatty in the crowd and he was playing with his computer again. It was so obvious he was watching me, because I know he hates basketball and who would want to watch our team anyway. The rest of the crowd was from the other school, lots of moms. Mine was apparently too busy, again.

Emily and her fake friend Janet came and cheered us on. It was pathetic and embarrassing hearing them cheer, "Put Ziggy on!"

I spent the rest of the day at Hiroki's house. We had sushi and his mom was very polite again.

Hiroki asked her heaps of questions about Takeshi Shibuya, but she didn't seem to know much about her own younger brother. She said he left home at 14 to go to a special school for gifted geniuses and after that she lost contact with him.

He apparently went to Tokyo University and topped every class. He graduated when he was 17 and started researching robotics after that.

She didn't know much about the Toyota Company, seeing as they had moved to Shanghai 10 years ago and rarely went back to Japan to catch up with their family.

Sunday

I'm still wondering about Takeshi Shibuya. I'm also trying to figure out what Mr. Brown and Mr. Smith are up to.

Hiroki, Tree boy and I went to the outdoor basketball courts to get some much needed practice, but we spent most of the time talking about a plan to uncover the truth.

Hiroki said he'd take his digital camera to school tomorrow so he could document evidence. Tree boy also had a good camera on his mobile phone, which he could hide easily. We all agreed that once we get some video footage of Mr. Brown using the computer, we'd show Miss Wood and see what she knew. Maybe she would help.

It's a good start.

That night I asked my mom about Dad and all she said was, "He always wanted what was best for you."

She'd said that before. I was too tired to argue with her so I just went to bed early.

Friday

This is Hiroki Yamaguchi reporting for Sigmund Zhou. A few days ago Sigmund went missing again. We were worried and called the police but, strangely, nothing was done. We were starting to think he was kidnapped again when something extraordinary happened. Sigmund has the ability to actually transfer his soul into other bodies. He did this again, but this time he didn't transfer himself into another human. At the moment he is occupying the body of a really big cockroach, and he can't, for some reason, change back.

His real body is in my room, sleeping safely next to my bed. Sigmund told me to take his body here, and he also told me to write everything down that happens in this diary, so here I am.

Sigmund didn't go to school on Monday because it was far too risky for a cockroach to go, and he could have been squashed. He played it safe and stayed in his room where his body is being kept safe.

Sigmund is a very clever cockroach, you know, because he managed to call Tree boy's mobile phone. When it called, Tree boy couldn't hear anything on the other end, but he knew the number was Sigmund's. He called me right away and we both went to Ziggy's house.

The strange thing was, Ziggy's mom just thought he was asleep, or sick. So we both went up to his room and couldn't wake him. That's when we found the cockroach. I almost stepped on it and Tree boy actually wanted to kill it, I mean Ziggy, but he flew around and landed right on my nose.

I looked at him and he did a basketball shooting motion to

try and give us a clue. He then flew to the phone and landed on the nine key, we watched as he tried to signal the letter 'Z' with his head and then flew to the four key and pointed to the 'I'. We didn't realize this, but Ziggy was trying to spell out his name. I was thinking it was some kind of super intelligent insect. Tree boy, however, still wanted to kill him.

He then flew into my ear and I heard his voice. It was very faint, but I could just hear him say "Ziggy!" and then "It's me Ziggy! Don't kill me!"

Then he flew back to the phone. I told Tree boy and at first he didn't believe me. Who can blame him for that?

I had an idea. I got Tree boy's mobile phone and then set it to loud speaker and put it in front of the cockroach. I dialed Tree boy's number on Ziggy's phone and picked up the phone. We could instantly hear him.

He yelled, "Hey, nice one Hiroki! Smart move!"

He sounds like Mickey Mouse when he talks, but I'm already used to it.

So Ziggy explained everything to us about how he could Jump and couldn't jump back. It was very strange listening to a cockroach talk for an hour.

After that we came up with an emergency plan. As long as Ziggy stayed a cockroach I would take care of him. I am feeding him every day and making sure he stays out of trouble. I'm sure I'm never going to forget this.

I promise to keep you safe Ziggy. I will report every chance I get.

Monday

This is Hiroki, reporting for Sigmund Zhou. Today I took Ziggy to school because he wanted to keep up to date with all his classes, even though he's still a cockroach.

I now have a walkie-talkie and have made modifications to it so that Ziggy can talk to me when he's hiding in my bag. That way I can hear him all the time. When the earpiece started working he called me a genius.

In English class Ziggy wanted me to give Miss Wood a message saying 'I miss you'. He crawled out of my bag just to see her. I quickly pushed him back in before anyone could see.

I helped him read from my Science, Math and English books and, I'm sorry to say it, but Ziggy, you are really bad at Math.

Tuesday

Ziggy told us to stick with the plan, so we did. Kane and I videoed Mr. Brown and Mr. Smith and I think they know that Ziggy is at home. We recorded their conversation and Ziggy asked me to transcribe it, so here it is:

Mr. Brown: So he's inactive?

Mr. Smith: Yes, we need to report this soon or they'll come looking for him

Mr. Brown: I'm sure he will activate himself again soon, our monitoring device is working well enough, no glitches to date

Mr. Smith: This is true, but we need more data on his progress or our positions could be terminated.

Mr. Brown: Toyota needs our expertise at the moment. We are getting close to finding out how Sigmund performs a leap.

Mr. Smith: We must locate him as soon as possible, or we'll be stuck here forever.

They both work for Toyota! This information excited Ziggy and he flew around the room for almost an hour. He's a naughty little cockroach.

No, I'm not erasing that part, Ziggy.

Wednesday

Emily asked me about Ziggy today and I said that he'd be back at school soon. It sounded strange lying to her and I was nervous, but my mom had taught me to always be polite when you are explaining something to someone. I always bow and use a nice voice. In Japanese we use different words when we are being polite, like Onegaishimasu: please.

Whoops! I'd better stop talking about myself, after all this is Ziggy's diary. He told me to write this letter for Emily:

Dear Emily,

I'm sorry I haven't contacted you in a long time but I've been very sick. I really like you and I want to continue hanging out with you at lunch with the others, but I think we should just be friends. I think I'm too young to have a girlfriend, but don't worry, you'll be the first girl I ask when I'm older!

See you soon,
Ziggy

I felt bad giving her the letter, and what made things worse was that she read it in front of me and started crying in front of everyone at lunch.

Ziggy was poking his little cockroach head out of my bag and he told me after that he felt really bad about it all.

When we went back home he actually cried too. It was really strange hearing a cockroach cry into a mobile phone. I'll never get that little chirping cry out of my head.

Thursday

Nothing much happened today. I lied more for Ziggy and tried to teach him some Math.

Ziggy, you have a lot to learn!

Friday

Ziggy is still a cockroach. I've been studying him closely with my magnifying glass and I've noticed he has little green spots all over him. I'd never seen a cockroach with green spots before so I googled it and found out some crazy information.

Apparently there has been a huge new discovery of a cockroach that looks exactly like Ziggy! It is named the Zular roach and I read some reports from farmers saying that thousands of them flew down like rain in southern Texas. Some other farmers reported that they saw a bright flashing light in the sky and suddenly their crops were filled with these cockroaches. So I guess that's what you are Ziggy, a Zular roach. A brand new species!

Saturday

Hiroki reporting again... It's hard work looking after a Zular roach, but when it's your best friend you have to make sacrifices. I missed the basketball game today because Ziggy asked me to spy on Mr. Brown again, so I did. I saw him using that computer device again. He was looking really worried and was sweating heaps.

Afterwards I found out Kane had actually played. He even scored 12 points! Mr. Smith must be losing his mind, or maybe he's too busy thinking about something else? I also heard that we lost again 54-31 and our record now stands at 0-5. Basketball is a difficult sport.

Monday

Ziggy, I apologize for missing my entry yesterday but I had no choice. My mom forced me to study and stay home. I kept Ziggy safe in my bag the whole time and last night I even tried to wash him. He was too scared and flew out of the bathroom as soon as I turned the tap on.

Today Emily was asking a lot of questions about Ziggy. She really likes you Ziggy, but she's very strange.

She said, "I need to know Sigmund Zhao's whereabouts immediately, Hiroki! If you have any information please verify it with me!"

Her voice was deeper than usual and her eyes appeared fierce and wild. I didn't know what to say and after a few minutes she went back to her silly, girly self. I think she might have two personalities!

NOTE: Ziggy appears to be growing more green spots.

Tuesday

Christmas Eve. Christmas is here and I don't feel like celebrating.

Today everything went wrong. It was very, very bad. Mr. Brown asked me about Ziggy and I, of course, lied and said I didn't know a thing.

He asked to see me at lunch and I foolishly went ... with Ziggy still in my bag!

When I got there, Mr. Smith was there too and both of them were holding those computer devices in their hands. Mr. Brown pointed his computer to my bag, it flashed and the inside of the bag became visible. They could see him trying to hide behind my books. Then Mr. Smith grabbed my arms and Mr. Brown reached in and grabbed poor Ziggy. He was screaming so loud I could hear him! It was awful.

They took him and told me to go to class, there was nothing I could do. I'm so sorry Ziggy, I failed. I'm the worst friend ever. I promise I'll get you back even if I have to fight them both! I'm a black belt in Karate, you know!

Wednesday

The worst Christmas ever! No Ziggy, no holiday!

I went to school feeling empty and kept looking into my bag expecting to see Ziggy, but he's gone.

Kane and I followed Mr. Brown and Mr. Smith around wherever we could, but it was hopeless. They kept disappearing whenever they turned a corner. We would hurry to catch up and they would be nowhere in sight.

I don't know how someone so fat like Mr. Brown can be so quick. Maybe he has some sort of magic power?

Emily could tell something was wrong. She looked really worried and kept asking me about Ziggy. I just kept lying to her, saying everything was OK.

Meanwhile Kane and I started working out a plan to get Ziggy back. We spent the whole day brainstorming ideas, but none of them seemed possible.

My mom kind of cheered me up and made us a big Christmas dinner. I got some Playstation games too, but I'm still really sad.

Thursday

Hiroki reporting, still no sign of Ziggy. I went to his house after school to see if his body was OK and he seemed fine. His mom was also strangely calm. Sorry Ziggy that might make you mad.

I told her Ziggy is in trouble but she didn't believe me and just said, "It's OK Hiroki, Sigmund is in good hands!"

She must know where he is! She didn't even seem to mind not having her only son there at Christmas! Well, I'd better not write anything bad about her, after all, this is Ziggy's diary.

I'm still so worried. I hope you're OK Ziggy. When you change back we're going to find out what's going on with my uncle and the Toyota Company.

Friday

My Uncle, Takeshi Shibuya wrote me an email:

To Hiroki,

How's Shanghai? I'm planning to go there for business this year so I'm sure I'll visit you and your Mother then. Maybe I can answer some of your questions at that time.

My company has been given authority by the Chinese government to build robots for the military, so I need to teach a lot of new staff how to use the machinery.

I look forward to seeing you soon,

Your uncle,
Takeshi Shibuya

This is great news, Hopefully Ziggy will be back by then and we can get some answers.

Monday

My Mother had me studying all weekend so I missed the game again. I heard from Kane that Mr. Smith didn't even show up and they played without a coach. They lost 8-64, that must be a record!

We had English today and I told Miss Wood that Ziggy had gone missing, and that Mr. Brown and Mr. Smith know where he is. She looked at me shocked and said, "I will get him back for you Hiroki, he misses you, but still doesn't remember anything."

Now, I like Miss Wood but what she said was really weird, I can't figure it out.

Tuesday

I'M BACK! Sigmund Zhao reporting! It feels *so good* to be me again! I see Hiroki has done a brilliant job. What a great friend! I thanked him over and over again, he almost cried when I turned up at school back in my normal body.

Before I get into all that, I need to write what happened to me first:

Mr. Brown and Mr. Smith are working for Toyota and for some weird reason they were saying Takeshi Shibuya is their boss. They put me in this strange box and it had all these green lights in it. I could hear them walking somewhere, and then they opened the box. I was in a white room, probably the same one from when I was abducted. I heard Mr. Brown say, "He's already developing his rebirth abilities and can leap at will, he's making good progress."

But then Mr. Smith said, "Yes but it appears that he still doesn't remember anything. We are failing our primary goal!"

They attached some wires to my cockroach antennas, pressed a few buttons on a machine, and I was suddenly in my room again. Happy to be human!

I felt so energized; I couldn't stop jumping around my room. I ran downstairs and gave mom a hug and all she said was, "Oh Ziggy, you're awake,' as if I'd only slept in or something.

But I'm learning to expect that sort of thing from Mom. Sometimes I think she's from another world.

I ran outside with my basketball and just kept running around the streets, dribbling between my legs. I ran to the basketball court and played for hours. I couldn't get tired!

So now I can't sleep at all and I'm just sitting here thinking about everything.

Description of Primary school:

As I lay in bed awake, my brain goes into overdrive. I started remembering primary school. For some strange reason, the memory feels so distant. It was only last year but it feels more like … thirty years. Which is impossible?

Memory:

Flashes of playing soccer in a grassy playground. Cheers from little girls watching on the sidelines. I have new shoes, a present from someone special. Who from? Not mom. I fall over and graze my knee in the mud. I cry and my hat falls off. Everyone stops playing. They point at me, some are laughing, calling me Freak boy! I run and cry more.

That is an old memory, I'm sure of it, and it's definitely me. Why can't I remember anything else about before? I'm sure with all this new found energy I'll remember more. After all, this is the first time I've written down a memory ever!

Wednesday

I'm back at school, hat on, and everyone is still staring at me again. I've figured out one thing sitting in Math class, I've realized Mr. Brown probably isn't out to harm me. He and Mr. Smith seem to know a lot more about me than anyone else, so it's about time I get some answers from them, directly. I'm going to ask Fatty tomorrow when I have Math tutoring.

Emily is not a happy girl. She was yelling at me today like some weirdo.

She said, "You may regret severing ties with me Sigmund, I have a very highly connected family you know, please reconsider your decision!"

Since when did she use words like that? Hiroki wrote earlier that she was asking me about me, sounding like a grown up, using all those big words.

I'm glad I broke up with her, but now I have to deal with her following me around like a freak!

Once again, I'm not sleepy at all.

Thursday

Last night I studied ALL NIGHT for the first time ever! Those Astronomy and Physics books that Mr. Smith gave me suddenly seemed interesting. I read them for hours. All the information seemed to fill my head and stay there! I might actually have a chance at passing a test soon.

I went to school still feeling energized and couldn't help but smile all day. Emily asked me why I was so happy but I couldn't really explain it to her. She'd never understand.

I was happy to see Miss Wood again, who seemed quite pleased to see me too. She even gave me a hug in front of the whole class and looked right into my eyes and said, "I missed you Ziggy."

It must have been really weird for anyone else in the class, but Miss Wood didn't seem to care. I think she really likes me.

After the hug, Hiroki later told me, I went red. I could hardly concentrate. I kept staring at Miss Wood, those blond curls and those big eyes ... long eye lashes. She's so beautiful. I can't get her face out of my head.

I've just realized it's the last day of the year! Aren't we meant to have a holiday? I guess our school is different.

Friday

A new year, a new me!

With more energy, I can play basketball better than ever! I was a defensive menace! My shooting was still horrible though. Mr. Smith was actually impressed too.

Afterwards he told me, "You are progressing really well Sigmund, have you been keeping up with your studies."

I told him I'd finished reading four chapters (which was pretty amazing for one night) then, I knew it was a good chance to ask him something, so I did.

I asked, "Mr. Smith, why am I so important to you and Mr. Brown?"

He answered, "Your well being is everything to us Sigmund Zhao, and your progress is even more important."

He was about to say something but stopped and reached into his suitcase. Out came the computer, like the one that we had stolen, it was flashing red. It started buzzing like a mobile phone. Then it was flashing like a siren on a police car. He pressed some buttons and put it back into his suitcase.

He said, "We'll discuss this later," and rushed off before I could find out more.

Mary Jiang also seemed pleased with me. She had this proud look on her face and she even sat next to me at lunch. I didn't mind because it made Emily sit with Janet.

I asked her what was up and she just said, "Sigmund, you are so special," then hid behind a comic book, which I realized was Spiderman, so it was obvious she wasn't reading it. What girl reads

Spiderman anyway? Anyway, she's not the type.

I got home today and found my mom sitting on the kitchen table, juggling fruit, nothing seemed to worry her; she was in her own little world.

I asked her why everybody was always telling me what to do and why was everybody so focused on what I was doing, and she replied with a smile, "Because you're so special."

It was, exactly, the same thing Mary Jiang had said earlier! Weird!

I guess I am special because I'm the only weirdo with two green things sticking out of my head.

Monday

I skipped the weekend diary entries because something amazing happened to me. I was outside the whole time playing basketball! Yes the whole time! I'm talking over forty hours straight. I had breaks for water of course, and snacks, but the rest of the time I was ballin' … and I'm not even tired now!

I did actually sleep a few hours after it, which was more than I had slept in over four nights. I can't believe I can do this, it's fantastic!

I was starting to put my hand up in science class today. I was answering questions and getting them right! The strange thing is Mr. Smith didn't even look surprised at all. The same cannot be said for Math. I'm still the worst Math student alive and Fatty doesn't like this. It's stressing him out. Maybe Mr. Smith and he have some sort of bet going with the Toyota Company to see who can make me better. I don't know? It's possible.

No English class today, so I didn't get to see Miss Wood. That sucks.

Tuesday

Miss Wood gave me that smile again today. Those lips and teeth look so good. It's almost impossible to read anything in class. I often look up from my work and catch her looking back at me. She smiles and sometimes even winks! I'm sure she likes me. It's crazy, I know, because I'm only twelve years old, but I really think she does.

Emily pushed Hiroki out of his seat in Science and sat next to me, huffing and puffing the whole time. She is quickly becoming my least favorite person to hang around, but I still want to try and be her friend. If she would stop acting so weird maybe it would be easier. Poor Hiroki had to sit up the back with stinky Troy Wu! I heard that boy hadn't showered in weeks.

I got home today and Mom was cooking pancakes. The smell was awful as she was burning them all.

She said, "Isn't it fun using a frying pan? It's very slow but you get to see the whole pancake forming. It's a classic kitchen appliance you know Ziggy!"

That's her being a weirdo again. I ate burnt pancakes and lied to her saying they were delicious.

That night the voice in my head finally returned and it had a lot to say.

The UPA (United People's Army) was formed in 2029, originally to combat the first foreign invasion which began in 2028. All the nations of earth decided unanimously to unite their military forces in an emergency counter attack. It took three years for the world's leaders to agree to terms; however their main concern was saving the planet from further destruction. Differences of opinion were set aside to focus on more important endeavors.

These steps would see the world's governments uniting in the years to follow and histories of war were soon forgotten in order to battle the new threat. The Toyota Company was then given full power in the military to construct their new technology. This was highly sought after by the UPA so Takeshi Shibuya, president of Toyota, instantly had a very strong influence. The Toyota Company soared.

Toyota constructed military weapons to defend against the invaders. At first these weapons were deemed useless against the powers of the enemy. The Zu...

Wednesday

I fell asleep writing last night which is why I stopped mid-sentence. I wonder what I was going to write. The Zu... something that starts with Zu, I don't know. I haven't heard the voice in my head today and it's usually just random information. Anyway, I've got other things to worry about.

I talked more with Mary Jiang today. Maybe she's not so weird. Maybe she's just following me around because she's got no other friends? She is definitely different to other kids though. Her hair is amazing. All those curls bunched up above her head make her look heaps taller. She's actually about Hiroki's height I think, and that's really short, even for a girl.

She told me, "Watch out who you talk to here. You can't trust everyone you know."

Which is some good advice considering what has been happening to me. It's almost as if she knows everything. Later, I asked Hiroki and Tree boy if they had told her anything and they said they hadn't told a soul, weird. I've got other problems. Mrs. Wang was asking about the History presentation I did in term one.

She said, "Sigmund, after hearing about Takeshi Shibuya and robots last term I thought you were just making the whole thing up, but I did some research and there is actually a Takeshi Shibuya working for Toyota, in robotics, in Japan!"

This is something we already know. I just nodded and she wouldn't let me go. She said, "How did you know this? Did you find it out on the internet and then make up a story from it?"

She was smiling when she asked me those questions and seemed very excited. I told her 'No' and asked her if she knew anything else about it too.

She looked shocked and said, "I'll get back to you Ziggy. This is very interesting, indeed."

So after thinking about it for a while, I realize Mrs. Wang might be able to help us by gathering information on Toyota. She definitely seems more normal than Mr. Brown and Mr. Smith.

Thursday

I went to the English staffroom this morning. I couldn't wait to see Miss Wood, even though I had English second period. I was up all last night again, my brain spinning around in circles, thinking about her. I wrote her another poem. Here is the final version.

I like English now so much
You teach it well,
A gentle touch
Sometimes it's hard
To stay on track
Even if I sit up the back
I see your eyes
And feel your smile
Then I try,
To write a while
But you seem to match
And attach to my brain making,
My poems' style

I typed up the poem on the computer and handed it to her.

She smiled and said, "Oh, thanks Ziggy, I've been waiting for your next one. You are really turning into quite the poet you know."

That made my day. I felt so proud hearing it. I strutted around school that day like a king.

Maybe I can become a poet? I love writing poems, but they are mostly for Miss Wood. Who else would want to read them? But, I guess, she is my English teacher so she would know a good poem when she sees one.

She doesn't feel like a teacher though. She's becoming like a friend, a really, really, good friend.

I saw a new teacher today in the English staffroom and he was sitting next to Miss Wood. He had Spiky black hair and wore a very expensive looking suit. He was smiling and I didn't like it. His teeth were way too white and perfect for me.

I saw Tree boy play basketball and he's getting better. He could actually bounce the ball a few times before losing it, and he could shoot hook shots! It won't be long until he's better than me.

I got home and actually studied Math. I studied for eight hours into the night, until I got bored of it and started drawing robot designs again.

Friday

I had Math tutoring again in the morning. I got a few answers right without even really trying. He still didn't seem impressed.

He told me, "Study more, you need to progress faster."

Again with the pressure, I wish we would just relax for a change. I must be the only student he ever thinks about. It's so strange.

In Science I was answering even more questions, probably because I read all of our textbooks six times already. The stuff on gas, liquids and solids was boring already. I was talking about the periodic table and comparing elements like sulfur and and phosphorus and asking Mr. Smith about metal extraction and electrolysis.

Hiroki was looking at me, confused. At lunch he asked me, "Hey, since when are you so good at Science. You've memorized the periodic table already."

I had no reason to lie to him. He had already saved my life once and had taken good care of me when I was a Zular roach, so I at least owed him the truth. I told him how I couldn't sleep and was studying every night. He was impressed and asked me if we could study together tonight. So he is here now. He is not studying though; he's taking a break reading some Japanese comics while I write this.

Saturday

Hiroki put in a good effort studying science with me but fell asleep around two in the morning. When he woke up at eight he was shocked to see me still sitting at my desk, reading.

He said, "You really can study all night. It's amazing!"

And I'm still not sleepy. It's great having all this extra time to myself. Come to think of it, I can do anything at night. I could go out and explore Shanghai! I could jump! I haven't jumped in a while because of the whole Zular roach disaster, but I think I'm ready now.

We had a game today verses Livingston International again and lost. I sat on the bench, once again, with Hiroki. Emily was watching us but this time Janet was there. She wasn't cheering either and I saw her just staring into space like a zombie. She's gone all weird since we broke up. I'm worried.

Mary Jiang was also watching our game. I saw her hiding in the back corner behind some parents from Livingston. I could see her curly mess of hair sticking up from above them.

She can't stay away from me, I wonder why?

Monday

I missed Sunday because I stayed over at Hiroki's place last night and Saturday night too. His parents thought it was a bit strange because it was a school night. I guess my mom is different. She basically lets me do anything.

We had sushi again. His parents really are nice. We just happened to get a call from Takeshi Shubuya last night too and I asked to talk to him straight away.

I asked him if he knew me and he said, "I'm sorry I don't know any Sigmund Zhao, but I'm coming to Shanghai next week, so I'm sure I'll have a chance to meet you as you are Hiroki's friend." His English was very good.

So all I can think about now is meeting Takeshi Shibuya. I'm so disappointed he doesn't know me but there must be some reason I keep hearing his name in my head. Maybe I'll show him some of my pictures, and then maybe I'll find out how this is all connected.

Some good news, I had my last Math tutoring lesson this morning! Probably forever! Mr. Brown told me that we have a test on Friday, so I can prove myself then.

Mrs. Wang spoke to me again after History class, she said, "Ziggy, I want to arrange a meeting with you this week. I think we need some special help for you."

So I figure she thinks I'm crazy. She could be right; I might as well talk to some professionals to find out. Maybe Mom should too, she seems crazier than me!

Is it all real?

I've done strange things
I've seen the other side
I've looked in the mirror
I ran away to hide
Myself in a secret
Wrapped up in the truth
My only constant is you
The crazy lies are true

Tuesday

My meeting came sooner than expected; Mrs. Wang took me out of Math class (no complaints) to meet two friendly men who always smiled. I knew I couldn't tell them everything, so I just told them about the Toyota Company. They asked me how did I know and I said, "I don't know, I just do."

They arranged to meet me again and Mrs. Wang was looking happy.

I saw that rich looking teacher again, walking with Miss Wood. They were laughing and chatting like old friends. I wonder where he came from. Miss Wood seems to enjoy being with him, a little too much. I don't like him.

In English I asked her who he was and she said, "Oh that's Jerry, although you should call him Mr. Lee. He's a really good, new teacher. He teaches English to children who don't speak it well."

I didn't like the way she was talking about him. I changed the subject and talked about poetry. I managed to talk to her for the whole lesson, while everyone else just talked or did nothing. Hiroki, of course, studied.

At the end of class she said, "Oh, I just missed the whole lesson!" Then she smiled and nudged me in the shoulder, saying, "It was worth it though, hearing you read some poetry is much better."

So I was smiling all day. She actually prefers talking to me over teaching! Me, some weird little kid with antennas.

Hiroki said I need to careful with her, but I can't stop now. She's the most beautiful woman in the world and she enjoys talking with me … and there's nothing wrong with that!

Wednesday

Thinking of you again
Your hands and your fingers
Have touched me before
Or was I asleep
You hair smells of memory
A spell or my destiny?
Your words come back to me
Like spring on the snow leaves

I wrote many poems for Miss Wood last night and I read poems by Sylvia Plath over and over again. I love reading Sylvia Plath. I don't know why but I feel I can relate to her, even though she was English and a lot of her poems are really depressing.

Thursday

Emily has become my shadow. I've often noticed her watching me out of the the corner of my eye. She doesn't look happy, and once I saw her making these strange faces. She was moving her eyebrows up and down really fast. It was freaky!

Friday

The craziest thing happened today. I jumped, twice, and I feel really tired now because of it.

The first time I jumped was in the Math test. Even after all the studying I'm still hopeless at Math. When Mr. Brown told us to start the test, I freaked out and my mind went totally blank. I tried to look at the first question and couldn't concentrate at all. After about 15 minutes of trying to figure out the first answer, I decided to jump. I jumped into Mr. Brown's body, but he didn't have the answers with him, so I stood up and said, "OK I need everybody to stop doing the test and study English, after all we know English is way better than boring Math."

I walked around the room as Fatty and collected every one's unfinished tests. I even took mine and saw myself slouched down in my chair, sleeping.

Hiroki knew what was going on but didn't say a word.

I stayed in Mr. Brown's body for the rest of the class and everyone started reading poetry or writing English essays. The bell went and I changed back.

I saw Mr. Brown looking at the tests with a big frown on his face.

I realize now that I made a huge mistake. Everyone is going to fail and it's all my fault. I feel so guilty, I know I shouldn't have done it but I panicked. Even Hiroki probably failed! His mom and dad will be so angry because they are used to him getting at least 99% in everything!

The second time I jumped today was after school. I was thinking about Miss Wood and that new teacher when suddenly

I was in Starbucks, looking at her. She was wearing a beautiful red dress.

Not having a clue what to do, I went to the bathroom. There I found out I was the new teacher, Mr. Lee and I wasn't impressed. I frowned in the mirror, showing those perfect white teeth. I flexed my muscles to see that Mr. Lee was also very strong. I went back outside and asked Miss Wood why we were there.

She said, "Well ... you invited me for coffee, remember? Jerry, you are acting weird all of a sudden. Is everything OK?"

It was a date. My Miss Wood was on a date! But I knew I could do something about it. I said, "I have to go, this is a mistake. What about Ziggy?" I ran out of Starbucks. I ran down the street and was dodging bikes and scooters on Xietu road. I stopped at a crossing and jumped back into my own body.

I don't feel guilty about my second jump. I thought Miss Wood really liked me but I guess she doesn't. Who am I kidding? I am kid ... and she is a beautiful woman. She should go on dates, there is nothing wrong with that. Except I'm so jealous!

Saturday

I really can't get this Jerry Lee guy out of my head. I've been imagining them going on dates, holding hands, laughing together. I try not to but I can't stop, I even imagine them kissing!

To get my mind off him I went to Hiroki's and found out Takeshi Shibuya would be arriving that day. But the strangest thing happened; we were playing PlayStation games when there was a knock on the door. It was Mary Jiang with her huge hair and she was puffing, all red in the face.

She told me, "I really need you to come with me now. It is extremely important!"

I had no reason not to trust her. She took me on the subway all the way to People's Square. There, surrounded by thousands of people she said, "I just wanted to show you this beautiful city. Isn't so classical? Look at the architecture in the buildings."

I have no idea why she took me so far just to look at buildings. After that she forced me to eat ramen noodles with her and then, finally, we went back. She was very bossy the whole time and even held my hand when we walked through the crowds in the busy subway stations.

When I got home I called Hiroki. He told me Shibuya had already left and would be leaving for Beijing tonight. So I missed my chance to meet him. Hiroki asked him about me, but he said he didn't know me. He also told me that he was talking a lot about the Toyota Company and the deal they have with the Chinese government.

I can't help but think Mary knows something.

Sunday

I'm not feeling so jealous today, probably because I've got loads of other stuff on my mind.

Firstly, Emily called me six times today, five of which I ignored. The first one, I answered.

This is what she said, "I really need to start rebuilding my relationship with you. It is extremely important for me and my family to secure our future. Please allow us more time to grow and flourish into what we are destined to be."

Her voice was deep and it freaked me out, so I just said 'Bye' and hung up.

Monday

Fuqian high is getting really weird. I don't know what's going on. All I have is two friends and Miss Wood to count on. Everyone else seems out to get me. Maybe I'm paranoid.

On Hiroki's suggestion I did some more research on the Zular roach in the library. I got some books on cockroaches and I've already read them all. I don't know why, but I like cockroaches, I can't remember thinking much about them before, but seeing as I can actually be in one, I think I need to know a little more about them. Apparently the Zular roach is a special kind of cockroach. A lot of research suggests that it never eats, and it can fly for hours without getting tired. It's a good thing Mr. Smith is looking after my Zular roach. He told me today, it's been sleeping the whole time. I asked him why and he just said, "That's just what they do when they are not being used."

I guess he knows I can jump!

Notes on the Zular roach:

Scientists claim the Zular roach is "The most intriguing scientific discovery of the decade!"

They are studying them in the USA, Australia and New Zealand.

No information available about Zular roaches in China.

Tuesday

Mary Jiang was following me around again today. She's like my security guard. Timmy Tang even tried to trip me over in the hallway and Mary actually pushed him over. Some grade nine kids laughed at him, it was funny seeing a tiny little grade seven girl push a big grade eight idiot over. He went all red and walked away trying to act like he didn't care. The dude must be pretty frustrated by now, he just can't win.

Mrs. Wang was once again asking about Takeshi Shibuya in History. She said, "Sigmund, I've found out a lot of information about Toyota Robotics online. I'd like to meet you again, maybe at the start of next term, and I'll have some of my friends there to meet you."

I just nodded and acted like I would go. I guess it wouldn't hurt to have another meeting.

Last night I read a lot. I also drew some more robot designs and wrote this poem for Miss Wood.

Lost In The Woods

The flower I search for
Seems so far away
The wind is strong
And the sky is grey
I'll bring you sunshine
And water your pedals clean
But there is a stairway beneath you
And a nightmarish dream

I am a seedling
And you are in full bloom
Deep in the earth
I search for your room

Wednesday

I'm happy again. I had English today and I was so pleased to see Miss Wood. She had some fantastic news!

She said, "Ziggy, I'm so sorry I didn't tell you about Mr. Lee. Really you have nothing to worry about, he's just my friend. I know I shouldn't have gone out with him, it's just I get bored waiting around, and he is such a classic 2000's guy. It's just so retro talking to him. I promise I won't do it again. I know how much I've hurt you and I'm deeply sorry."

After hearing that, I just smiled and stared at her. We talked for ages and she once again skipped half the class. Hiroki wasn't impressed, but Kane loved it and gave me the thumbs up at the end of class. Mary didn't seem to mind either.

Emily's face looked like a beetroot!

Thursday

School isn't important anymore; all I need is Miss Wood.

Feed the starving

Your words bring water
To thirsty deserts
Your fragrance is a cure
To the polluted restless
Your voice settles down the angry
And pacifies the war mongers
Your eyes say everything,
Will be alright

I can't stop thinking about her. I'm so glad she isn't Mrs. Wood, because then I'd be so lost. I probably wouldn't even go to school. She's the best!

Friday

I also need to learn how to play basketball, I suck! I think after all this time, I'm actually getting worse! Mr. Smith doesn't seem very interested in our team anyway. He missed seeing Kane do three really cool lay-ups because he was talking to Mr. Brown again. What are those two up to? Probably something to worry about. Hiroki even got a three pointer and he didn't even seem to care. I think we need a new coach.

I forgot about how bad a player I am when we had English. Miss Wood actually sat next to me and asked Hiroki to read out the poetry all lesson. She and I both clapped after every poem, smiling and laughing the whole time. I showed her my Lost in the Woods poem, which I typed up and printed out yesterday. When she read it she looked a little sad and I actually thought she was going to cry.

She said, "This is beautiful Ziggy, I can't believe how good this poem is! You never used to write, I love it!"

I'm thinking about what she said now. I never used to be a poet? Maybe she knew me when I was in primary school, maybe she can tell me why I can't remember anything. I'm going to ask her when I get a chance.

Term 3

Three weeks have passed since my last entry. I was once again abducted and tested on and missed my whole holiday again. I can't understand why they always do it when I don't have school. It makes no sense; next time I hope they do it when I'm about to do a Math test.

This time around they strapped my antennas up to tubes and it felt like they were sucking my brains out. The people were wearing masks and I had no idea where I was. All the walls were white and there weren't any windows. I kept falling in and out of sleep, and they injected me with heaps of needles. They barely spoke and whenever I tried to speak I felt my head sting like it had been bitten by a giant mosquito. It hurt more this time. They were pulling my arms and legs and after a while I felt taller.

It went on forever.

I heard a machine humming and beeping behind me but I didn't have the strength to look around.

Finally they blindfolded me, put me in a car and drove me back to my place. Mom, once again, didn't seem worried and just gave me a pat on the back and said, "I missed you Ziggy," like I'd just been on camp.

I ignored it and went up to my room. I slept for three days.

Monday

I had missed so much this time. It's really annoying me. I was so hungry today; I got two pizzas delivered in Miss Wood's class. She of course let me eat them, and watched on like I was her pet puppy.

She seemed really worried about me and even bought me a bottle of orange juice. She said, "You know, I got this because it's your favorite."

She was right too, I do like orange juice, but I can't remember ever telling her that. Weird, she must have found out from someone else.

Hiroki kept apologizing to me. He said he and Kane were looking everywhere for me over the holidays. He even thought I might have gone all the way to Japan to talk to Takeshi Shibuya.

Emily totally embarrassed me at lunch. She cried and yelled, "Sigmund you must update me constantly on your whereabouts. I was extremely concerned!"

She grabbed me so tight I couldn't breathe. In fact, I thought I was going to pass out, so I pushed her away. That was the wrong move because she slipped over, hit the table behind her and flipped right over it. What made things even worse, she was wearing a short skirt so everyone in the cafeteria saw her green undies. So many kids were laughing their heads off.

Another crazy day at Fuqian high, I'm glad to be back!

Tuesday

The voice was back in full force today and it didn't shut up either. I couldn't concentrate so all I could do was write everything I heard. SEE BELOW.

The invasion was too much for the UPA. Even the improved technology built by the Toyota Company wasn't enough to defend against the ongoing attacks. The way in which the alien forces attacked was quite varied and almost always started with attempted communication. They already had the ability to communicate in Earth's major language: Chinese, and put across a request before attacking that usually consisted of, "We seek the resources and landmass you possess, please enable our race to use it for our own purposes to extend our empire."

The UPA would not negotiate with invaders therefore the attacks soon came. The alien forces were swift and superior. They often used forms of telekinesis to separate UPA soldiers from their vehicles to dismantle the newly made robots. They did this from outer space so there therefore not risking being hit by nuclear blasts.

Wednesday

Reading back what I wrote yesterday freaks me out. I'm hoping I'm crazy and the voice is just my imagination, because if it is real and in the future there is an invasion, I'll be terrified!

Miss Wood asked me today if I was looking forward to my birthday. Strange thing is, I can't remember when it is. Is that normal?

I asked Hiroki if he knew his birthday and he just laughed at me and looked at me as if I was crazy.

I wonder why Miss Wood knows my birthday and I don't.

As soon as I got home I asked Mom and she said, "It's next week of course."

But I can't remember the date, so I still don't know what day it's on.

Thursday

Seeing as I haven't slept in three days I've had more time to write poetry. This one is my favorite. They're all for Miss Wood of course.

You know

You know so much
My mind and touch
You see through me
With eyes of love?

How do you know
All of these things
Are you an angel?
With hidden wings

When I smell your hair
And see your smile
I can't help but think
And stare a while

Are we good friends?
Or something more
An open heart
And opened door

Friday

Back at basketball training again and everyone was looking at me like I was a stranger. Wally and David think I'm a freak and Jimmy wouldn't even pass me the ball when I was totally open. Hiroki and Kane hadn't changed at all. I'm glad I have them to talk to.

Mary Jiang was with us again at lunch. Her hair was fuzzy and crazy as usual. She's not afraid to sit next to me, which I don't mind. I guess she's cool in her own way. Emily is the shadow now, always listening and lurking behind us.

Mary told me, "It would be a good idea if you stay away from people you think are acting strange. Always stay around groups and never go out at night."

So now that she told me not to go out, I can't stop thinking about it. I'm awake almost every night with nothing else to do except read and study, and I've done plenty of that. I wonder why it's dangerous for me anyway. Why am I so important?

Saturday

I went out tonight and had the time of my life! Completely ignoring the warning Mary Jiang had given me.

First I'll write about my day:

We had a game and played Fudan High; they are the best team in the league. We actually played well for a change and scored a little. Mr. Smith even put me on and I scored four points!!! A new season high. Hiroki even got time on court and scored two points! We were so happy, even though we still lost; we were singing all the back home. Kane made up this funny rap about us and it went something like this:

Fuqian is shocking the world
Rocking the shots and impressing the girls
Fuqian is surprisingly good
With a bunch of lunatics hitting the hardwood

We kept rapping it over and over again and it was driving Kane's parents crazy.

Not much else happened. Emily called me and asked me to see her and I stupidly said yes because I was in a good mood.

Now I can write about my crazy night. I went out all by myself and wasn't scared at all. I took the subway to Xujiahui and went to an internet cafe. Everyone was playing a game called BioWars in a tournament, so I joined in. It was my first time ever playing it, but I was so good at it. I killed everyone else and won the whole tournament. At the end everyone applauded me and I got this cool free pass to the internet cafe which lasts a year. This basically means I'm going back there as much as I can.

It feels great to actually win something for a change.

Sunday

I met with Emily at the front of Jing An temple and once again she was wearing a dress that looked way too grown up for a 12 year old. It was a black lacy traditional Chinese dress and she even had matching black high heels on. Her hair was tied up in two buns with two black chopsticks. All this effort to impress me.

She took me by the hand straight away and dragged me into a tea shop. She ordered the most expensive tea and paid before we started drinking. I saw at least two thousand Yuan in her matching black purse.

She said in a deep commanding voice, "Sigmund, I think it's time you know the value of our relationship. So much depends on our future."

I was trying to ignore her, enjoying the hot tea. She kept going, "Our future will be so grand in this new found land. We may someday rule the empire. Do you know how marvelous that is Sigmund Zhao?"

By this stage I had had enough. I decided to tell her exactly how I felt. I said I didn't want to be her boyfriend EVER and didn't even want to be friends. I also said, "You are a little crazy for me anyway." Which I totally regret.

She went bright red and smashed the tea pot with her fist. Hot tea went everywhere. I ducked a huge wave of tea; luckily it missed me and splashed all over the floor behind me. Glass was sticking out of her fingers and she wasn't even crying. She was just really angry.

That was when I made a run for it. I ran so fast to the subway, it was like Olympic speed! I was way too scared to look behind me. I got to my station and ran back home.

When Mom saw me she knew I was scared and locked the door behind me. She told me to go to my room and I've been here since. I heard her talking on the phone to someone, but I didn't want to know who it was.

So ends the worst date of my life.

Monday

Today was my birthday and I didn't even realize it until I had breakfast and Mom gave me a present. I opened it and found a computer inside. It reminded me of the computer that Mr. Smith and Mr. Brown had been using and when I looked inside I even saw the brand name Toyota!

She said, "You've needed this for a long time Ziggy, I think it will help make things a lot clearer. I can also keep an eye on you with it."

I hope I can get BioWars on it.

Today was a good day. Emily was away so that helped a lot. I wasn't freaked out as much. Also, Miss Wood surprised me in the cafeteria with a big ice-cream birthday cake. It had sparkling firecracker candles on it and even had my name written in chocolate topping!

Everyone sang happy birthday and Miss Wood gave us all big cans of orange juice. When the bell went she whispered in my ear, "I also got you this," and slipped a little box into my pocket. She said, "Open it at home, it's a secret."

So, I have just now opened it and now I'm staring at this shiny green ring. It fits perfectly on my left ring finger and it lights up the whole room when I turn off the lights.

So now I'm 13 years old. Weird thing is, I feel so much older.

Tuesday

A teenager does things differently at school. I took my new computer with me and wore my ring. Miss Wood smiled at me and said, "Oh you're wearing our ring, it looks so cool Ziggy!" and fuzzed up my hair.

Hiroki was impressed with my computer too. He was even more blown away by the fact that it was made by Toyota! It was exactly the same trademark as Takeshi Shibuya's!

I was trying to figure out my computer all day and still am now. It looks black but it kind of reflects light when I tilt the monitor. It's almost paper thin and hardly weighs a thing. The keys flash green when I type on them and the loading screens have the Toyota trade mark. The opening window has ten folders and I can open them by touching the screen. Three folders are in some weird language I've never seen before, but the other seven have loads of documents about Toyota products. Something is telling me the voice in my head isn't just my imagination. I really don't think this computer is just a toy.

There are even designs of the flying water powered car that I had drawn and presented to my history class, and there are heaps of robot designs and information. All of which I had heard and written down earlier in the year!

The even more interesting thing about my new computer is the TakeshiNet feature that I found flashing at the bottom of the computer screen. I touched it and heard a woman's voice say, "Connecting to TakeshiNet-you are now connected."

I was in the middle of the library when I figured this out so everyone looked up from their books and frowned. To make things worse it started humming and suddenly my mom popped up on the screen.

She said, "Hello, Ziggy, nice to see you're figuring out the computer, take your time reading all the documents. Well, I've got to go, I'm trying to make coffee again, it is so difficult!"

I spent the rest of the day reading Toyota documents.

Wednesday

Emily was away again, thankfully. I still can't believe how she acted at the tea shop. Freaky!

I had completely forgotten about my second meeting with Mrs. Wang and those friendly people. In history class she whispered in my ear. "I've scheduled a meeting for you this afternoon. Is that OK with you Sigmund?"

I realized then that I'm probably not crazy and going to see those doctors would only complicate things more. I needed an excuse fast, but I couldn't think of one, and once again found myself stupidly saying, "OK, I'll be there."

I was freaking out at lunch and Hiroki, who was sitting next to me eating sushi, asked me, "What's up Ziggy, you looked worried?"

I had kept my visits with Mrs. Wang a secret, but secrets hadn't solved any of my problems, so I told him everything. Kane and Mary happened to be sitting with us too, so they heard it all.

When I finished Mary stood up and her mass of blond curls brushed my face. She said, "This can't be good Ziggy, you can't go and we must stop Mrs. Wang from investigating any further. It is crucial that she doesn't learn anything from you."

Suddenly Mary Jiang sounded like a teacher and all we could do was stare at her with our mouths hanging open, nodding.

So Mary, apparently, went to see Mrs. Wang after lunch. I'm not sure what happened but she seemed determined to keep those doctors away from me. When we were sitting in Math class, last period, Mrs. Wang knocked on the door and asked to see me in the hallway. I noticed her eyes looked different.

She said, "I've made a mistake Ziggy, we won't be having anymore meetings, see you in class."

Her voice was deeper than usual and I can't help but wonder what Mary had said to her.

Thursday

Not much happened today. I realized I'm already up to the grade 10 science books and reading every night is really helping. I can still remember almost everything in the books and Mr. Smith even said, "I'm noticing a progression in you Sigmund." Whatever that means.

Even though I try to read the math textbooks, whenever I do, I start to think about Miss Wood, and then I end up writing poetry.

Here is my latest:

Why this ring?

Why this ring?
You said it's ours
It lights up the night
Like our love powers
For you every hour
Of every single day
Growing stronger still
Blue skies once grey

Giving me safety
In times of danger
I can't believe
We were once strangers

I want to sing my poems to Miss Wood or maybe even rap them. That would be cool, but I'd probably make a fool of myself.

Friday

Miss Woods' nose and mouth are so cute. I was staring at her the whole time in class today. She has these perfect red lips that look even better when she smiles. Her nose is small and pointy and it moves when she talks.

Once again I'm going on and on about her, but I can't help it. She's a fantastic single woman, who happens to be very beautiful, and I get to see her almost every day. And I know she likes me. It sounds crazy but I just know it!

Thoughts and whispers

You are big
I am little
You are older
I am younger
Why why why
Can't things be different
I think of us
As kindred spirits

Saturday

All I did was study science and work on my computer today. Funny thing is, there aren't any games on it. I asked Mom and she just laughed and said, "Oh honey, it's not that sort of computer, it has a lot of data and monitoring programs, you can also laser equip the CB2 if you want?"

I had no idea what she was on about. So I just read more documents on it.

I completely forgot we had a basketball game and called Hiroki later to find out we lost to Livingston High again. Mr. Smith was there and the score was 21-109! How could they possibly score that much?

It was too cold to go outside and play on the outdoor courts so I stayed in and Mom cooked fried rice. It was burnt but she still seemed to enjoy it anyway.

Sunday

I touched the TakeshiNet trademark on my computer last night and suddenly I saw Miss Wood smiling back at me. It was embarrassing because I was wearing my monkey pajamas so I quickly put a jacket on. She was still smiling when I got back.

She said, "Hello Ziggy how's the studying going?"

I replied, "Good" and asked her why she was on my computer.

She said, "Oh I'm always online, you know, doing history research ... I mean English literature research for teaching, of course."

She sounded like she was joking but I couldn't tell.

The conversation didn't stop there. She wanted to talk and talk for hours. It was great and I noticed she had a huge mug of Starbucks beside her which is probably why she didn't get tired. We chatted until three in the morning!

I read her all my poems and she looked so happy to hear them.

She said, "I'm going to put them all into the official publications systems, so they'll never be forgotten. I know the tax rate is high but it's worth it to preserve your art."

I guess she meant she wanted to put them on the internet.

Monday

A 13 year old kid has to set an example for all the other 12 year olds in grade seven, but I found out from Hiroki that there are only two kids left that are still 12 and they are both girls. We didn't know how old Mary was, so we asked her.

She said with a strange look, "Oh I'm actually 14, um… I missed a lot of last year so I have to do grade seven again."

14? I can't believe it! She's tiny even though her hair is massive. Hiroki is short really but he's 13. So I guess I'm the youngest.

Maybe Mary is lying though.

Tuesday

I went to that internet café again last night and played BioWars for six hours straight. I already have the most powerful gun. I'm killing everybody else online with ease. I don't why but I'm so good at it. It's already starting to get boring. I guess now I need to find a new game.

Miss Wood sat next to me again in English. She said she couldn't resist talking to me and I read her some of my poems. Once again the rest of the class did whatever they wanted.

I'm starting to worry about what the rest of the class thinks. I heard Janet say she wanted to have one of the Sylthia Plath poems explained but Miss Wood was way too busy enjoying my poems!

Wednesday

Today Mr. Brown said we have a midterm test on Friday, so I spent the whole afternoon and evening revising all the math units in the textbooks. I had them all memorized by about eleven pm. I'm determined not to fail another test!

No more time to write.

Thursday

I studied and tested myself for the math test tomorrow. I think I'll do just fine. I'm far above everyone in the class, except of course Hiroki, the genius. He's topping every class we have together.

I helped Kane out a bit today and explained some algebra. He came over to my place and when he stood next to Mom, he towered over her.

She said to him, 'Oh I love your hair; it's such a reflection of the decade. I know you're making a grand statement to the world. Keep it up."

Once again embarrassing me, and freaking Kane out too.

We studied for hours until finally Kane fell asleep at one am. I'm going to keep studying.

Friday

I thought I was well prepared for the test but I didn't realize my computer is like a mobile phone. I was just starting the test this morning when it started vibrating in my bag. Mr. Brown told me to answer it so I picked it up and there was Miss Wood smiling back at me.

She said, "Ziggy, I just wanted to tell you I love your poems and I can't wait to hear another one!" then she blew me a kiss and winked!

That was enough to blow me right off track. I felt all hot and I couldn't concentrate. I tried to answer another question but it was hopeless. Miss Wood's pursed lips were cemented into my head and there was nothing I could do about it.

I actually ended up writing another poem and didn't even answer a single question. I handed my papers to Mr. Brown and he waved his head.

He said, "Still no progress Sigmund. What is it about Math that you find so challenging?"

I couldn't answer his question because I was still in my little world with Miss Wood.

Saturday

Seeing as I missed yesterday's basketball training Mr. Smith had another reason to bench me again. We lost again, of course, and I sat watching with Hiroki, bored out of our minds. When I got home I found a suitcase in my room and heaps of my clothes folded up. When I asked Mom about it she said, "Oh yeah Ziggy, I forgot to tell you, we are going to Beijing for two weeks, seeing as you haven't had a holiday in a while."

So I'm flying to Beijing for two weeks. No school!

Sunday in Beijing!

It was a short flight and seeing as this is my first time in Beijing, I'm very excited. Our hotel is great; it has a huge TV, a spa and a big bed just for me. Mom said one of the reasons she wanted a holiday was that she was tired of cooking. I didn't tell her, but I'm pretty tired of her cooking too.

We both relaxed all day in the hotel and ordered room service. We went out for dinner and had Beijing duck. It was delicious.

Beijing is very beautiful at night. The lights on the high-risers are like stars in the sky. Our hotel room is on the 31st floor so it kind of feels like we are floating in space on some sort of cool space ship. Sometimes it feels like the floor is moving too.

I brought my computer with me because I wanted to see Miss Wood, but she wasn't online today.

Monday

Today was so cool! We went to see the Beijing Ducks basketball team, it was awesome. My mom has planned out the whole two weeks and has tickets for so many things.

At the game, we were up really close to the court, in the third row. We could see everything and could even hear the players argue.

But I was even happier when we got home and I found Miss Wood waiting for me online. She even blew me a kiss again and said that she missed me!

Mom and I spent the rest of the day relaxing in the hotel. We both got massages and I sat in the spa for ages.

Tuesday

I was studying my antennas in the mirror this morning and noticed they are growing. They are at least 2cm bigger and I'm beginning to feel this lump on my lower back. I guess puberty is starting for me.

Today Mom and I took a boat ride around a beautiful river. I forget the name. There were heaps of old people with us and some of them were looking at me funny. I kept checking to see if my NBA hat was on firmly, and it was, but the people kept staring.

Wednesday

I actually slept last night. Maybe because I've got no textbooks with me and Miss Wood wasn't online.

Today we went shopping and I bought three new extra large hats. All NBA, because it seems that the NBA is the most popular basketball league in the world. I got LA Lakers, Chicago Bulls and Orlando Magic. They seem to be the most popular teams too.

Mom went crazy shopping and bought five new dresses, five pairs of shoes that matched each dress and five handbags that matched everything! I have no idea where she is getting all the money from. I'm sure she doesn't have a job.

Thursday

More relaxing today in the hotel. I saw Mom typing away on her computer in some other language. I guess that's her job. I decided to write some more poetry for Miss Wood. The best teacher in the world.

Teach me

Teach me more
Teach me now
Teach me how to
Tame this love

Teach me right
Teach me wrong
Teach me how to
Sing our song

Teach me friendship
Teach me pride
Teach me how to
Stay alive

Teach me always
Teach me plans
Teach me how to
Be your man

Friday

Today was the best day here so far! We went to the Great Wall and it was magnificent. We walked for hours and hours and stopped at one of the highest parts. I took some paper with me and drew a sketch of Mom in front of the wall.

We walked all the way back down and were exhausted. We ate dinner at a great seafood restaurant and now we are back in the hotel, resting our aching feet.

Saturday

We went to Tiananmen Square today and to some war museums. I looked at a lot of World War 2 weaponry and felt like I had studied them before. I was fascinated with the rifles and the bayonets. They were so long and even though they were behind the glass I could somehow guess their weight. I'm sure I've held one of them before but I can't remember when. In fact, I'm sure I've held many guns.

I loved looking at the old swords too. The long thin Kung-fu weaponry impressed me the most.

Once again Mom had planned another great day!

Sunday

I already miss Miss Wood. Miss Cherry Wood. That's her name, Cherry. Her birthday is on the 30th of July, why do I know this? I'm sure she hasn't told me. I think she loves eating chocolate ice-cream too and loves to read fantasy novels for hours at night. Maybe she told me and I just forgot.

Anyway, today was another cool day in sunny Beijing. It's pretty cold, but still good weather for holidaying. If I was in Shanghai I'd probably be stuck in the middle of some boring Math class with Fatty. Instead I'm here having the time of my life.

We went and had a look at the Bird's Nest Stadium today. Mom said that the 2008 Olympics were there, but I couldn't remember seeing it on TV.

Mom said, "The fact that it was all man made in such a small time is amazing!"

My mom loved Beijing; she was always going on about how quickly buildings were built and how much risk was involved in making them.

Monday

Today we went to The Forbidden City. This took up the whole day and despite its fascinating size and beauty I felt something bad was going to happen as soon as we entered the huge red gates.

Mom was going on and on about the ancient history of the buildings when I started feeling weird. I felt my antennas twist around and bend backwards, so I looked behind me. I saw a flash of a black dress vanish behind a corner.

Later, when we were in the Emperors throne room, my antennas twisted back again. I couldn't see much because there were so many people, but I caught a glimpse of that black dress again.

On the trip back to the hotel I kept looking back behind us. It was driving me crazy.

I can't sit down now because I'm wondering if someone is really following me.

Tuesday

Our visit to the Confucius temple was spoiled by a very unexpected reason to jump. Mom and I were looking at a statue of Confucius when my antennas twisted and bent backwards again. I turned around to see that same black dress floating behind a tree. I saw an old man standing in front of the tree and I jumped into him as fast as I could. I ran around the tree to find Emily, panting and puffing.

I asked her, "Why are you here?"

She didn't say a word and just ran for it. I tried to chase her but I was an old man and I started coughing and feeling my heart hurt, so I jumped back.

Mom was trying to wake me because I was lying on the ground in front of the Confucius statue. A crowd of tourists had already gathered around us.

I stood up and guided her out of the temple to see if the old man was OK. I found him sitting on a bench, looking confused and puffing.

I told him I was sorry, but he didn't know why I was apologizing of course.

So Emily is in Beijing and is following me around for some reason. It's creepy to think that she has come all this way to see what I'm doing.

Wednesday

We went to an art gallery today but my mind wasn't on the paintings. I'm going crazy trying to figure out why Emily is following me. I still haven't told Mom about it.

She was going on and on about these Chinese artists and how important they are, but I could hardly hear her. I was busy looking around every corner for Emily. I didn't see her anywhere though.

She's already spoiled my whole holiday! Why is she so obsessed with me? Next time I see her I'm not going to stop until she tells me the truth.

Thursday

No sign of Emily again today. We went to a big IMAX movie theatre and watched Avatar in 3D. I heard from Kane that it was a good movie and he was right! I loved it, but I was still taking off my 3D glasses every minute to look at people getting out of their seats, thinking they were all Emily.

Things got better in the afternoon when Miss Wood reappeared on my computer. I remember every word she said.

"I miss you so much Ziggy, I hate being so far from you. I really want things to go back to the way they used to be, but I know I have to wait."

She was going all red when she said it and I thought she was going to cry. She said, "You have to try and remember everything Ziggy, that's the key, once you remember it all, we can be together again!"

I'm really confused now. I want to believe her but I don't know what she means. What does she want me to remember? Primary school? That seems like forever ago.

Friday

Our last day in Beijing was a good one. We went shopping and Mom bought me so much stuff. I got an MP4 player, a Nintendo DSi, 5 new pairs of jeans, 3 new shirts and a leather jacket. Mom called it *Retail Therapy*, and it works!

Now, I'm already feeling better after playing my Nintendo DSi and listening to some cool new rap music. I can't complain really, I got 2 weeks off school in the middle of term.

I got 12 new games with my Nintendo DSi as well. I love Super Mario and I've got three cool NBA games too. So that'll help me learn all the players' names that Hiroki keeps going on about. There is this one game, World War 3, it's kind of like BioWars except you're fighting aliens instead of army men. The first time I played it I couldn't die. I'm so good at it that I almost know what's going to happen next. I picked up all the new weapons and killed at least 200 aliens! I think I'm a computer game genius!

Saturday

I'm back in Shanghai and I can't wait to get back to school! I called Hiroki and he said our team won! It's amazing and I'm so jealous, I wish I was there to see it. Apparently Jimmy and Wally played really well and the score was 54-49, against Shanghai International! The only bad news was Mr. Smith didn't let Kane or Hiroki play at all.

Not much happened at school when I was gone. Hiroki tried to talk to Janet a few times (MEGA CRUSH!) but all she did was talk about Emily. She's apparently really worried about her and they haven't talked in months.

They used to be best friends in first term but Emily changed into a complete weirdo and has been ignoring her all this time.

Change

Why do people change?
Strange how people don't
Stay the same
Under lights
They look different
Why are they so strange?

Monday

Back at school and back to normal, but I guess I'm hardly normal. I've noticed the lump on my lower back is getting bigger and it's getting hard to even sit down. I asked Hiroki if he had a lump and he said he didn't. I guess he's a pretty small kid still and his voice is still really high, so maybe it will grow later?

In history class Mrs. Wang was back to her normal self. She set us a new assignment. We have to write a report on a famous person from any time period. I've already started researching on the internet. I really want to write about a war hero, I haven't decided who yet.

Everyone was pleased to see me at school. Emily wasn't around so I couldn't ask her anything. I asked Janet about her and she seemed really sad, she didn't say much. Hiroki was excited because she sat next to us.

After lunch Hiroki kept saying how much he loved the sound of Janet's laugh, but we hadn't heard that in a while.

I remember Janet and Emily always being together, but that was a while back.

I didn't have English today but Miss Wood actually came into my Math class and asked to see me. Fatty just said, "OK, go ahead, take your time."

We talked in the hallway. She gave me a big hug and I gave her the Teach Me poem that I had written in Beijing. She was so happy to see me.

Tuesday

I was up all night reading history textbooks, mostly on World War 1 and 2. I found some interesting stuff on Chairman Mao and thought about writing my assignment on him. Mrs. Wang would love that, but I'm still undecided.

I played that World War 3 game and finished the whole thing already. Way too easy!

Today Mary Jiang was acting weird. She kept giving me this weird smile. She said, "You're becoming a man Ziggy," and giggled like a little girl watching cartoons.

Miss Wood told our class that we would be studying poetry all next term! Somehow I think it has something to do with me. She gave me a wink after telling the class, so I guess it's pretty obvious. I wonder why she's doing all this for me.

I got home this afternoon and thought the kitchen was on fire. It turned out, Mom was just trying to cook pizza! We ate black, disgusting pizza and it took heaps of brushing to get the horrible taste out of my mouth. The really strange thing was, Mom thought it was delicious.

Wednesday

I found this huge weapons document on my computer and looked at it all through math class. I completely ignored everything Mr. Brown was saying and he didn't even seem to mind.

There is a massive amount of information about guns, missiles and even rocket launchers! The dates on the guns must be all wrong though, some say 2025! How can that be possible? This Double Automatic Missile launcher says it's made in 2026!

Anyway, its cool to look at, better than Math. I looked at this self-reloading blaster (SRB) and really felt like I'd seen it before. Maybe it was in BioWars or something?

Thursday

Last night I went out to that internet cafe and played BioWars again. After a few hours I had already killed everyone in the building. I could tell what the other players were going to do next and I'd just shoot them from long range before they had a chance.

At about 4 AM a group of men circled around my computer and one of them tapped me on the shoulder. He said, "Hey you are really good at this, you should enter the Shanghai championships next month." He gave me a card that had *'The Championship of BioWars'* on it.

I went to sleep for about half an hour when I got home and dreamt I was in the World War 3 game. I don't remember it clearly, but I was using a self-reloading blaster to kill this scary green alien.

At school I realized the end of term is coming up. This probably means I'm going to be taken away and tested on very soon. It totally sucks!

Friday

Hiroki, Kane and I are now trying to come up with a plan to avoid me being captured. Hiroki, being the genius that he is, has already got a pretty good plan.

I left school early today to prepare, in case they come early. Kane was a big help because his father just happens to own a Chain factory. He brought a really long steel chain and a welder to my place and we all got to work.

Hiroki and Kane chained me up pretty well and Kane welded the chains to a telegraph pole outside my room window. That was part one of our plan finished. The second part was food supplies. Hiroki and Kane went to the nearest Lawson and came back with a huge carton of Coke, a box of potato chips, loads of jelly beans, chocolate and a big container of sandwiches. I wore my leather jacket to keep warm. So I'm set now.

We made sure I could walk back and forth to the toilet but that was as far as I could go, which means no school for a while.

The two of them then went downstairs and told my mom that I had arranged a week of at home study with Miss Wood. They reported back soon after and Mom actually believed the lie!

So now it's late and I'm sitting here in my chains with my computer next to me, munching on some yummy potato chips. I've got everything I need now, books, paper, my MP4 player and my Nintendo DSi.

Saturday

I'm already bored and it hasn't even been 24 hours yet! One thing I am doing a lot of is playing World War 3. I can't stop. So I've just been sitting here eating chips, drinking coke and playing computer games. Pretty fun stuff.

Sunday

Now I'm really bored. I keep calling Hiroki and Kane just for something to do and they are already sounding annoyed.

I've already mastered all 12 games on my Nintendo DSi, so I've been reading documents on my computer. There are a lot to get through, so I guess they are keeping me busy.

Monday

I'm starting to regret our plan. I called out to Mom so many times today but I think she's gone out. She hasn't answered me all day and I'm starting to worry. I'm too worried to write anymore.

Tuesday

I jumped today, only because I was so worried about Mom. I jumped into her and found myself in the math staffroom of all places. Mr. Brown and Mr. Smith were in front of me and they were both holding computers that looked exactly the same as mine!

Mr. Brown asked, "Grace? Is everything OK, you just stopped mid-sentence and went silent. What do you think we should do about Sigmund's progress?"

I was shocked and still couldn't say a thing.

Mr. Smith said, "He seems too concerned with irrelevant things like basketball and Cherry is distracting him with all this poetry business."

That was all I could take so I jumped back.

I realize now that Mom must have been meeting with Mr. Brown and Mr. Smith and they've been talking about my progress. She hasn't been pressuring me to study so I can't figure out why she's talking to them.

Wednesday

I heard Mom come home and she came up to see me. She was so shocked she screamed when she saw all the chains around me. She yelled for ages and called me crazy. She even tried to break the chains, but of course couldn't, she's not superman.

After a while she gave up and went downstairs. She returned later with a plate of bacon and eggs, apologizing. They were burnt, but it was still a great change from potato chips and sandwiches. She stayed with me all day and now she's asleep on my floor.

A long time after…

They came for me as expected that day. I woke up to find three men in white suits cutting my chains apart with knives that glowed green! I wasn't just going to let them take me this time. I jumped into one of their bodies and punched one of the other men as hard as I could in the face. I then jumped into his body and punched the other guy.

Mom was up and was just standing there, looking worried, letting it all happen.

I managed to put few bruises on their faces but one of them pulled out a huge pair of tongs and ran to my body. I saw him clamp the tongs over my antennas and then I was suddenly in my own body again, unable to jump.

They then all ran over to me and injected me with needles.

I woke up in that white room again, on a bed with a machine beeping away next to me. My antennas were hooked up to all these wires and I couldn't move.

Our plan had failed.

I was in the white room forever! I think this time they wanted to do way more tests because they were talking more and writing more stuff down on clipboards. They injected me with loads of drugs and they were so strong this time I thought I was growing. My arms and legs felt like they were stretching down the end of the bed. I woke up later and realized I must have just imagined it because my legs were the same stumpy size.

Later on there were more men in white suits standing around writing stuff down. They didn't say anything, so I couldn't figure out what they were doing. Probably *'monitoring my progress'* as Mr. Brown would say.

They started injecting needles into my antennas too, which had me worried. I'd fall asleep when they did this and have really weird dreams. I'd be jumping really high in the air around a strange forest that had trees with bright purple leaves. I could jump high above the tree tops and see a night sky filled with stars. There were also three moons!

The injections continued and I went in and out of sleep like a baby. Finally, after what it felt like forever, I woke up in my bedroom. Mom was by my side with a glass of orange juice.

She said, "Good to see you are awake Ziggy, you have someone very special waiting to see you." She gave me a big hug.

Miss Cherry Wood was waiting at my bedroom door with that beautiful smile. She was wearing a red dress that I swear I've seen before. I felt like kissing her so much, but I didn't even have the energy to lift my head.

She said, "I missed you Ziggy,' and gave me a hug. Her hug felt different to Mom's."

Mom left us alone, which was weird, and we talked for hours. She talked about school, poetry, basketball, and I told her everything I'd been through in the last three terms at school. She told me I'd already missed the first two weeks of the forth term and Mrs. Wang had told her I'd missed the history assignment too. But it was OK because she said I could have a two week extension, so I'd better get started soon.

We were talking for so long that I fell asleep half way through a conversation.

I woke up and found a note:

I didn't want to wake you as you need more rest, see you at school soon!

Cherry Wood

Under her name was a love heart!

I didn't have the strength to jump out of bed, but I felt like celebrating. Instead I just ate more of Mom's burnt pizza and fell asleep.

Cherry Wood

I was lost in the woods
Cherries on all of the leaves
Not wanting to be found
Red cheeks and red sleeves
The men in suits searching
Calling out for me in the distance
I hide in her leaves
The smell covers my ignorance

Wednesday

Two more days was all I needed and now I'm fine. I went to school with my new Chicago Bulls hat, feeling lighter, but refreshed. I walked to school feeling the warm spring sun.

Hiroki and Kane were really happy to see me and were frustrated that our plan hadn't worked. I told them not to worry about it, it's over and there's nothing we can do about it. Time to concentrate on school! Our final exams are all next week, so I need to catch up on heaps of studying! I don't want to do grade seven again.

So now I'm actually worried about English. I heard from Hiroki that all of grade seven has to do the same English test! If that's true then our class will all probably fail because all we have been doing is reading poetry!

I asked Miss Wood about it today and she just nodded and said, "Don't worry Ziggy; I'm sure everyone will be fine. It's just a test, it's really not that important."

Hiroki is freaking out about it. He's trying to get all these other stories and reports from other kids, frantically. I'm sure he doesn't have to worry about math though, he's been topping that all year, that and history ... and science, not to mention all the other subjects.

So I only have five more nights until the Math test on Monday, so I'd better start reviewing!

Thursday

I studied math all night and I feel like a zombie. This afternoon Hiroki, Kane and I studied in my room for about six hours.

This is all I can write because I need to study more.

Friday

More studying and I think I've memorized everything I need for both math and science. I've got to start studying history.

Nothing else interesting happened today, except I noticed Mary isn't studying at all and doesn't seem worried at all. She was just watching us study at lunch with this weird, proud look on her face.

Actually, come to think of it, I've never seen her study or even do any work in class. She always seems to be just ... watching me.

The voice came back to me this afternoon, it said:

By the year 2029, the earth was bracing for a full scale invasion. The UPA was united in defending the earth the best it could and finances were tripled to make weaponry and artillery. All the funding from the police, navy and air-force were taken and spent on this effort and countries soon changed for the worse. When the Aliens were visible, fear spread across the public. Mass hysteria soon followed, causing economies to crumble. Huge corporations soon went bankrupt due to lack of staff and the crime rate doubled monthly. Terrorist organizations soon took control of several major cities. Most of the population became preoccupied with maintaining their own lives and weren't prepared for the invasion.

Saturday

I think I'm all set for the science exam considering I'm already finished reading the grade ten science textbook. I've also read about 10 books on Astronomy, not that I need it for the test; I've just really gotten into that sort of stuff.

No more time to write, I've got to start my history assignment.

Sunday

After 10 hours of reading and writing, I'm almost finished my history assignment. I chose Genghis Khan because he was a really powerful leader. His empire was the biggest and stretched all the way from Asia to Europe. Today, I wrote a lot of information about the weaponry the Mongolians used and drew details pictures of spears and swords.

I found a Genghis Khan document on my computer too and it said that Mongolian artifacts were found in northern Africa in the year 2018! Written scripts and paintings depicted a war between the Mongolian Khan Empire and the Christian converts in Cairo, Egypt. Historians had to rewrite a lot of textbooks when the carbon dating came back revealing the artifacts were from about the year 623AD. This meant the Khan Empire had extended all the way into Africa too!

But its 2010, so those artifacts haven't even been found yet.

Monday

The voice was back, only this time it sounded a little different. There was more emotion in his voice and he actually sounded sad. This is what he had to say:

The UPA were helpless to stop the alien forces from invading earth. Our once free and peaceful existence was short lived. They came in full force after our defenses were down. Their methods were ruthless. Entire neighborhoods were lifted out of their homes and placed in huge storage vehicles against their will. All nations were helpless to counter as the alien forces dismantled all our nuclear rockets.

Then they went for our resources and started sucking us dry. They brought in technology that was so advanced even our top scientists couldn't understand how they worked. The aliens used their hovering spacecrafts equipped with massive vacuum tubes to evaporate our uranium supplies in just days. Soon our oil was gone too and all the survivors could do was sit and watch as it all disappeared.

Our greatest fear was losing our limited water supply, but for some unknown reason, they left that alone in the initial invasion. Their plans were to extend their empire, so Earth, being a water planet, remained that way for their benefit.

The death rate was low. Luckily it wasn't their intention to murder and destroy. We soon came to learn that they needed earth greatly. Their home planet lacked a lot of the resources we had in abundance.

Tuesday

I managed to do pretty well in my science test, despite hearing the voice the whole time through it. When I handed it into Mr. Smith he gave it a quick look and was impressed. He looked up at me and actually smiled! I think that's the first time I've ever seen him do that!

I went home early today and finished my history exam. I couldn't resist and added the discoveries from the future. I even printed out the document from my computer and attached it. Mrs. Wang doesn't think I'm crazy anymore so it should be OK this time, I hope.

I had a memory today! I'm sure it was a memory. I was walking down an empty street, holding this huge silver gun. It was raining and there was lightening striking in the sky above me. Huge apartment blocks loomed over me with smashed windows and graffiti all over them. Trash and rotting food spilled and tumbled in the cold wind. I was on Nanjing road, but it had been abandoned.

I was wearing a gas mask and my antennas were poking through the top. The air was unbreathable. I had a flashing screen strapped to my arm that I used to monitor movement, I was searching for life. Suddenly the screen started flashing and beeping. I felt relieved at the possibility of someone else being here.

Then the ship came. Its speed was sickening; it appeared in a breath, filling the cloudy sky. Its bright shiny silver metallic hull filled the horizon, reflecting the apartments and the street. I knew that ship, it was coming for me. I had to run. Escape; get out of there, quick.

I turned and ran, clicking a button on my waist to activate my speed skates. The wheels sprang out and I glided around the corner onto Nanjing West. I called home base but there was no reply.

I felt the heat of the ship behind me. It was no use. I couldn't outrun the mother ship! Then the pain; tentacles gripped my antennas, lifting me up into the air. Blood fell like rain on the empty street. The blood was mine.

The weirdest thing about that memory, I think I had whiskers!

Wednesday

I felt really weird today. My antennas kept twisting around in my hat and I thought Emily was back, but I didn't see her. I was all hot and sweaty and my heart was beating hard. When I handed in my assignment to Mrs. Wang, my antennas shot up and lifted my hat right above my head. They then twisted backwards and Mrs. Wang yelped like a small dog. I looked outside the history staffroom, but no one was there.

Mrs. Wang just said, "Oh, it's OK Ziggy, I know you are different you don't have to be embarrassed. It looks like you've done a really good job on the assignment. I'll read it tonight."

So now I'm freaking out again, trying to study for my math test tomorrow. Could Emily be back? Is she going to do all her exams? She must be close because my antennas never lie!

Monday

I'm back and safe, all because of Miss Wood! So much has happened since my last entry. It was insane! I have to think back to when all the madness started.

It was a Thursday morning and I was about to start the Math exam, when my computer started beeping loudly. It was so loud it sounded like an ambulance siren!

Mr. Brown stopped eating a sandwich and walked right up to my desk. He took me by the arm and said, "Sigmund, you have to go now. You are in danger!"

My antennas started twisting and bending again and my hat fell off. Mr. Brown took me out into the front of the school and said, "Stay low to the ground Sigmund Zhao, I will get reinforcements immediately!"

My computer was booming its high pitched siren right across the sports field. I squatted down as low as I could and put the computer on top of my head. My ears felt like they were bleeding.

After a few minutes I felt a tapping on my shoulders. I looked up to see Hiroki. He said, "Ziggy, I don't think it is wise to stay here. Inside there are more teachers to protect you."

I trusted Hiroki. So we ran back inside and Hiroki guided me into the library. It seemed like a good idea, but as it turned out, it was a huge mistake. As soon as we passed the front desk we heard the doors shut behind us. We both ran back to them and tried to open them, but they were jammed shut!

Hiroki was starting to panic. He asked "What's happening?"

But I didn't have a clue.

We searched around the library to find ourselves totally alone. We were locked in and had no idea what to do.

I said, "Let's go to the Manga section!" because there was a big window at the end of the aisle.

So we frantically ran down the aisle and reached the window. I used to like looking out of that window, when I read comics. Then I saw something through it that will forever scare me. Emily was hovering in the air! She was flying around like a bird and was giving us both a smile that gave me a chill. She was wearing that same black dress. She flew down from high in the sky and smashed her fist right through the window!

Glass went everywhere. She poked her head through and said, "Ziggy, it's time for you and me to be together again!"

We tried to run, but just as we did all the comic books came falling down on us from the shelves. Some of them hit my head, hard. I dropped my computer and heard it hit the ground behind me. I saw Hiroki tumble to the ground, tripping over comics. More and more books came down on us, and then there was darkness.

I woke up to find myself tied to the bookshelf. Next to me Hiroki was also tied up, with bruises all over his arms and legs. I felt so guilty seeing him there with his eyes closed. I looked around but couldn't see my computer anywhere. Outside, it was night time and the playground was empty. A few florescent lights flickered above us and I could hear the ticking of a clock nearby. Other than that, the library was silent. Emily was nowhere in sight.

I tried to nudge Hiroki but he was just too far away to reach. I whispered, "Hey, Hiroki, wake up," but he didn't.

I heard him sigh and murmur something. I hoped he wasn't hurt badly.

Just then, my ring started glowing. The green light started as a flash then brightened and lit up the aisle. I moved the ring's light over Hiroki. Making sure he wasn't bleeding or anything. Thankfully, he looked OK.

I heard something move. Books from other aisles were hitting the ground. There was this slithering, hissing sound. I shined my light down the end of the aisle. There she was. This was her true form. Two long green antennas appeared around the corner of the aisle. Then she revealed herself in full. She was a beastly green thing with an oval shaped head. Her black hollow eyes came towards me. Her long green skinny body followed as if they were two separate things.

She said in deep, booming voice, "Ah, Sigmund Zhao, why did you have to make things so difficult? Don't you understand what is at stake?"

It sounded like Emily. She had used that voice at the tea shop when she smashed the tea pot everywhere. She continued, "If we are married, we can move quickly into higher royal positions, soon the entire empire will be ours! You see, it won't be long until the Emperor passes and then the throne can be yours and mine!"

She got really close to me. Her teeth were razor sharp and glowed silver in the light. Her breath was so bad I felt like vomiting.

Hiroki started to moan so I yelled, "Quickly Hiroki wake up!"

But it was useless. The Emily-thing wasn't finished. It said, "Don't you see how pitiful these humans are with their delicate bodies and primitive minds? Why do you continue to mingle with them when you know you are one of us?" At the time I had no idea what she was on about.

She got even closer to me and said, "Your birth mother was only the subject of an experiment that we implemented to breed out the human race. She was the first step in the *extinction* of the human race."

I felt hurt hearing that. I yelled at her, "Why do you have Emily's voice? She's human!"

"Emily? I am known as Ethius Impolius. That female human was just used as a vessel to get closer to you, Sigmund Zhao. You need not worry about her; she is sleeping in a hospital with her pathetic mother constantly by her side. You know of our most celebrated ability. Leaping from body to body is a wonderful power that I see you haven't forgotten."

It was making me angry, I yelled, "But why do you want me?"

Her black eyes doubled in size and she muttered, "Why do I want you Sigmund? Your father is none-other-than the Emperors' secretary and supreme guardian! Your bloodline has ruled the Zular people for centuries, you are royalty Sigmund Zhao ... or should I call you by your real name, Altarish Peglimith*!"

Hiroki was still moaning, his eyes still closed; I tried to reach him again but it was hopeless.

Emily, I mean Ethius, opened her mouth wide. I thought she was going to eat me.

I yelled, "I'll never marry you! You're a complete freak!"

This was a mistake. She screamed a high pitch blast that shook the windows.

She said, "Unwise decision Altarish. As I suspected you are still bound to that human female you seem so bent on wasting your life with. I won't allow you to waste your destiny on a human!"

Suddenly her antennas stretched high above us and came down, tangling with mine. She twisted them in a knot. The pain was so intense I felt like I was going to faint.

She screamed, I thought Hiroki would surely wake up, but he just moaned and his eyes stayed closed.

I thought I was going to die. I was thinking about how young I was. There was so much more to learn, more to remember. I had only just become a teenager!

She tightened her antennas. I felt the roof and walls swaying. Then, the whole library was spinning. It thought it was the end, but it wasn't.

My ring started flashing again. There was a huge eruption of sound behind us. The library turned a fiery orange and suddenly Ethius was gone. I looked down the aisle to see Miss Wood holding a huge silver gun on her shoulders, like some sort of future soldier.

She ran to us and looked straight at the ground. She yelled, "Where did she go?"

I looked down to see some glowing fluorescent green water. She got down on her hands and knees and peered under the bookshelf.

She yelled, "Ah, she's getting away!"

She ran back out of the aisle and I heard books falling in the aisle next to ours. I asked her what was going on and she came back with a jar. Inside was big, bright green Zular roach. I only realized later that it must have been Ethius!

Miss Wood relaxed and gave me a worried look. "Ziggy, you're safe now, my man is OK!"

She untied me, and then we both untied Hiroki and laid him on the ground.

Then, the best thing I could ever imagine happened. She lifted me up into her arms, looked deep into my eyes and kissed me. It wasn't just a little kiss. It was deep and passionate and it felt perfect. I knew those lips.

I forgot about the pain.

We kissed for a long time, until finally I asked her, "But you are my teacher Miss Wood, I'm only a kid, how can you kiss me like this?"

She just smiled and said something that made a lot of sense. "Ziggy, you're not really a kid, and besides, it's been way too long since we last kissed, I couldn't resist."

She kissed me again and grabbed my hand. The ring she gave me glowed brighter than it had ever done before.

I'll never forget what she said then, "There's nothing wrong with a married couple kissing Ziggy, it's perfectly normal."

That's right, she said married! At the time, my head was about to explode. I was about to ask her a million questions when Hiroki finally decided to wake up. She put her finger over my lips.

Hiroki got up and asked, "What happened? Where's Emily? Oh look, another Zular roach."

I knew what Miss Wood meant; we couldn't tell Hiroki a thing. He probably wouldn't understand anyway.

The three of us made our way out of the library. We were surprised to find Kane wondering around with a worried look on his face.

He said, "Great I finally found you guys, I've been looking all night. What happened?"

Before we could say anything Miss Wood said, "Just some Zular roach problems, that's all. I need to take the three of you home, before your parents call the police."

I smiled to myself as we walked out of the school. Miss Wood took us all, including Ethius the trapped Zular roach, in her car. We dropped Hiroki and Kane off at their homes first. When she got back in the car she held my hand all the way to my place.

I think just holding her hand is almost as good as kissing her; almost.

Out the front of my house, we kissed again. I remember now, that we have kissed before.

We could hear Ethius in the jar buzzing around, probably totally jealous.

I waved goodbye and she drove away.

I started writing this entry straight after, because I don't want to forget a thing.

* I have no idea how to really spell it.

Tuesday

I totally aced the science test and Mrs. Wang really liked my assignment on Genghis Khan. She didn't really understand the parts I added about the new discoveries found in Egypt, so I lost 20 marks for it. But I still got 70%, which is pretty good.

Both Hiroki and I got to take the math test, but we had to sit in separate rooms, seeing as he is a genius and all. I was going OK until the craziest thing happened. My ring started glowing again and I saw Miss Wood walk past the room window. She blew me a quick kiss and that was enough to blow my concentration off totally. All I could think about was kissing her perfect lips and I ended up not writing a single thing! AGAIN!

So I failed again.

I don't know what is going to happen after summer in grade eight. Mr. Brown might make me do grade seven Math again or he could make me do those horrible morning and lunch classes. I'm not looking forward to it.

I've been too busy to write, recently. Spending time with my wife!

Monday

I love the last weeks of the year at Fuqian high. The teachers basically let us do anything! All we did was play board games and watched movies. We watched Toy Story 3 today. I was enjoying it until suddenly I felt a sharp pain in my back. I put my hand down the back of my pants and found blood. I ran to the bathroom and Mary actually went in there with me. She wasn't scared to just walk right into the boys' toilets!

I slammed the toilet door and she was waiting outside. She didn't seem too worried though. The pain got worse and something pointy started sticking out of the bump in my back. It got bigger and bigger until finally a long green tail stretched out of it! Yep, I have a tail! I'm a complete freak.

When I had finished wiping all the blood off my hands and legs with toilet paper, I opened the toilet door to find Mary smiling.

She said, "Ziggy, you're becoming a man!"

Then something even crazier happened! Mary pulled out her tail! She had a long green tail, just like me! Then she pulled her hair down and I couldn't believe what I saw. She had antennas, just like mine! Two green feathery antennas sat staring back at mine!

She winked at me and, just as I was about to ask her a million questions, Hiroki walked in. She quickly covered her antennas up in lightening speed.

So I have a tail, and Mary Jiang is like me! I'm not the only one! When I see her next I'm going to find out everything I can. There must be a reason we are both at the same school.

End of the year!

I can't complain too much about grade seven, it wasn't all bad. I handled Timmy Tang and his so called gang, I went from not having a clue to reading grade ten science textbooks, I had a girlfriend who ended up being a freak and I just found out I'm actually married to my English teacher!

I'm straining my brain now trying to remember what happened before, but I still can't recall a thing. I'm making it my mission over the summer holidays to remember, so many people seem to be depending on me to do so.

I still can't forget what I heard Ethius say about my father too. Something about being the Secretary to the Emperor. What Emperor? Where? I need to find out and seeing as Miss Wood still has her in a jar, I'm sure I'll have a chance to find more out over the break. Maybe Mom doesn't know anything.

I want to remember my wedding! I keep staring at my ring and somehow I know Cherry is telling the truth, why would she lie about something like that?

This afternoon she even sent me a message on the TakeshiNet

I love u Ziggy. Can't wait to see you in grade eight, after summer

It's amazing! I read it over and over out loud in my room. Miss Wood loves me!

I saw Mary walking home today and when I was about to ask her something, she said, "Ziggy, I have to go away for awhile but I'll be back for the new year. I have a lot of things to take care of. I know you have many questions, but I can't answer them now. Please be patient Ziggy. I'll miss you!"

She ran off, without giving me a chance to even say goodbye. So I guess I have to wait until grade eight to find out why she is like me.

So I guess I'm finishing up writing this diary. It's been a crazy year but I survived, thanks to Cherry. I'm not going to write over the summer, I'm taking a well earned break from my entries. It's time to relax and concentrate on remembering.

I'll start a new diary when the new school year starts. Not really looking forward to grade eight though.

Signing off, Sigmund Zhao.

(Husband of Cherry Wood)

The Shine

So many questions
So many answered
Dreams came true
Memories remembered

A year of friendship
Hidden enemies
Eyes on me
Focused on destiny

Young body not mind
Finding new talents
Pressure from teachers
Exhausting my patience

The flame re-kindled
She draws near
Her warmth is relief
Extinguishing fear

I thought I was the only one
But I've discovered one other
She watches over me
And we hide undercover

www.ingramcontent.com/pod-product-compliance
Lightning Source LLC
Chambersburg PA
CBHW071150260626
47162CB00003B/991